MISSION
CATASTROPHE

Lincolnshire

Edited By Elle Berry

First published in Great Britain in 2019 by:

Young Writers
Remus House
Coltsfoot Drive
Peterborough
PE2 9BF
Telephone: 01733 890066
Website: www.youngwriters.co.uk

All Rights Reserved
Book Design by Ashley Janson
© Copyright Contributors 2019
SB ISBN 978-1-78988-225-4
Printed and bound in the UK by BookPrintingUK
Website: www.bookprintinguk.com
YB0396Q

FOREWORD

Young Writers was created in 1991 with the express purpose of promoting and encouraging creative writing. Each competition we create is tailored to the relevant age group, hopefully giving each student the inspiration and incentive to create their own piece of work, whether it's a poem or a short story. We truly believe that seeing their work in print gives students a sense of achievement and pride in their work and themselves.

Our Survival Sagas series, starting with Mission Catastrophe and followed by Mission Contamination and Mission Chaos, aimed to challenge both the young writers' creativity and their survival skills! One of the biggest challenges, aside from facing floods, avoiding avalanches and enduring epic earthquakes, was to create a story with a beginning, middle and end in just 100 words!

Inspired by the theme of catastrophe, their mission was to craft tales of destruction and redemption, new beginnings and struggles of survival against the odds. As you will discover, these students rose to the challenge magnificently and we can declare *Mission Catastrophe* a success.

The mini sagas in this collection are sure to set your pulses racing and leave you wondering with each turn of the page: are these writers born survivors?

CONTENTS

Isabelle Eve Croft (11)	57	Ruby-Ann Carter (12)	99
Harvey Michael Doona-Grummitt (11)	58	Emily-Jane Abigail Cowdell (11)	100
		Ryan Blanchette (12)	101
Kerisha Wahrd (11)	59	Ambra Bohoslawec (11)	102
Abi Tempest (11)	60	Stefan Fota (13)	103
Krystian Zdrojewski (13)	61	Matilda Rainford (11)	104
Jack Ashcroft-Day (13)	62	Scarlet Morris (12)	105
Maddison Turrell-Simpson (12)	63	Connor Young (12)	106
Daniela Lucan (11)	64	Angel Uzzell (13)	107
Bethany Chester (12)	65	Maddison Spence (12)	108
Isabel Smithett (11)	66	John Miller (11)	109
Wiktoria Segiet (12)	67	Gracie Rose Moore (12)	110
Faith Croft (13)	68	Olivia Briggs (14)	111
Katy Edwards (13)	69	Kaylah Nicholson (12)	112
Chloe Louise Buckthorp (11)	70	Sophie Hockney (11)	113
Oliver Giovannetti (12)	71	Amy Madison Sienna Esberger (13)	114
Brandon Thorold (11)	72		
Jake Humphrey (11)	73	Charlie Preston (12)	115
Charlie White (12)	74	Vinnie Pickersgill (12)	116
Lili-Mai Chardoux (11)	75	Lewis Smalley (13)	117
Faith Dixon (12)	76	Jaydee Millward (13)	118
Harrison Bower (12)	77	Ruby Shaw (12)	119
Tyler Dalton-Minter (11)	78	Alfie Bunn (11)	120
Justyna Bachowska (13)	79	Ellie Anderson (12)	121
Chanel Parker (12)	80	Faith Patton (13)	122
Morgan James Davis (12)	81	Carly Burnett (12)	123
Chloe Joyce Lowe (14)	82	Kai Wilmer (11)	124
Sophia Cerniaskas (12)	83	Layton Jay Foley (11)	125
Grace Walker (14)	84	Michael Denman (12)	126
Beau Scott-Davies (13)	85	Courtney Cash (12)	127
Sophie June Lowe (12)	86	Charlie Smith (12)	128
Aleysha Marie Smith (12)	87	Morgan Higson (11)	129
Lucy Wright (11)	88	Oliver Jamieson (11)	130
Alex Vidas Martinez (12)	89	Charley Burton (12)	131
Charlotte Sophia Ellis (12)	90	Freya Annaise Parkinson (13)	132
Kenzie Long (12)	91	Addison James Hopkins (11)	133
Jake Frost (12)	92	Tylor Jones (11)	134
Dylan Lee (12)	93		
Ella Headland (12)	94		
Sharn Rhianna Heyward (12)	95		
Isobel Morrison (13)	96		
Freddie Hardy (11)	97		
Josh Walster (13)	98		

St George's Academy - Ruskington Campus, Sleaford

Samuel Bowring (13)	135
Charlotte Burton (12)	136
Libby Gardner (13)	137
Louise Hirst (12)	138
Hannah Hicks (13)	139
Joseph Dean Miles Enderby (13)	140
Gracie-Leigh Jaggs (12)	141
Joseph Swann (13)	142
Olivia Rice (12)	143
Natalie Louise Howard (12)	144
Libby Curtis (11)	145
Grace Emily Hands (11)	146
Ben Bunting (12)	147
Jacob Doughty (12)	148
Chloe Hargreaves (12)	149
Abigail McMunn (12)	150
Joshua Lee Young (15)	151
Rhys Davies (11)	152
Kayleigh Abigail Holly Voase (12)	153

Andrew Carter (15)	168
Oliver High (11)	169
Maisie Lamingman (12)	170
Erin Gerry (13)	171
Anya Lynne Wright (14)	172
Robyn Angel Byrne (11)	173
Damon Corney (13)	174
Eve Ellie-Mai Gurbutt (14)	175
Lauryn Walker (13)	176
Martha Isabella Moon Walker (11)	177
Cerys Webber (14)	178
Summer Rush (11)	179
Phoebe Swann (13)	180
Jake Walkenden (14)	181
Tristan Robinson-Marriott (12)	182
Lexi Reid (11)	183
Sophie Jo Wright (12)	184
Carys Scott (13)	185
Jack Lawrence (14)	186
Dylan Jones (11)	187

The Priory City Of Lincoln Academy, Lincoln

Amy Wilkes (12)	154
Eloise Hall (12)	155
Faith Parker (12)	156
Kayleigh Clavin (12)	157
Lewis Meekings (12)	158
Katie Founds (12)	159

Winterton Community Academy, Winterton

Mya McVeigh-Judd (12)	160
Ellie Crampton-Pullan (12)	161
Harriett Hall (11)	162
Keira Ramseyer (12)	163
Lanny Barton (14)	164
Curtis Bailey (13)	165
Dylan Walker (13)	166
Erin Taylor (12)	167

Mission Catastrophe

It's the end of the world as we know it... The silence of the thundering volcano ached the humans' ears. The lightning and lava lit up their houses in seconds. Screams and shouts came from the injured. Struggling survivors searched desperately for their loved ones while others ran for their lives. The historical monuments were destroyed and nature had vanished. Earthquakes struck, separating individuals from their communities. Bombs like boulders came down with a bang! Bouncing impatiently, they killed some more. The poor infants cried for their families, not knowing what was to come. Their beautiful world was now gone!

Lauren Disney (12)
Barnes Wallis Academy, Tattershall

Sister Willow

She grasped the cross and started to chip away the wood, getting ready for what was about to happen. She crept to where the altar was and saw Mother Superior kneeling down with her hands clasped together. "Lord, forgive me for the sin I am about to commit," whispered Sister Willow. So Mother Superior couldn't hear her prayers.
Sister Willow silently tiptoed towards Mother Superior. Viciously, she stabbed the sharpened cross into Mother Superior's head, killing her instantly. The terrible threat was gone. There were only zombies in the kitchen now. Willow would deal with them later that evening.

Mia Lassmans (11)
Barnes Wallis Academy, Tattershall

Race Of The Gemstones

The fragment of precious emerald glowed - pulsating at a calm, steady pace. Obsidian's face, illuminated with the green light after being shrouded in shadow for hours, produced a small smile - an admirable feat considering the hardship he'd battled over the past months. He closed his pale, scarred hand around the gemstone. Drawing back his hand, Obsidian lifted the crystal from the pedestal. The sentries had allowed him entry, but he stayed alert. This was a monumental mission - if he succeeded, it could change the course of the entire war.

Obsidian strode away, encased in darkness once again.

Elise Field (12)
Barnes Wallis Academy, Tattershall

The Wicked World

One day, Lilac saw something rather strange. The birds weren't tweeting! Suddenly, an enormous storm rustled up and came nearer to the playground. The remaining people outside managed to get inside. The storm picked up houses and tossed them away. It was as careless as a vampire. Then the storm shot slime at Barnes Wallis, which made the academy fall on its side. The furious, raging monster lifted the overturned school and tossed it away, killing everyone. This continued for ages since the storm spread to other countries. Once life was destroyed and everything was gone, the storm vanished.

Zaynah Rashid (11)
Barnes Wallis Academy, Tattershall

Quakes

I rummaged in my pocket and retrieved my walkie-talkie. My hands trembled with fear... would anyone reply? I dropped my walkie-talkie and kicked some rubble. I froze and my whole body shuddered. No one would answer...

At that moment, the ground rumbled and I twirled around in fear. Not another quake! I scooped up the walkie-talkie into my hands and dashed towards some rubble. As I darted towards the rubble, the ground shook with rage. The floor vanished beneath my feet and I felt like I was freefalling into a gloomy abyss.

Thud! A noise...

"Hello?"

Albie Swift (12)
Barnes Wallis Academy, Tattershall

Werewolves

Brooke's subject yelped at the prick of the needle. Kidney disease needed to be stopped... End of. It was 3156 now. Cancer was gone. This was not! So, now he had to be monitored over three weeks. Effects had taken place. Fur. Fangs. Ears and... A tail! They were not human. Wolves. Werewolves. Mindless, aggressive werewolves. She had created man-eating werewolves. Death came closer to humanity. Brooke had to cure him... them. Shattered glass... screams and cries of her colleagues. The reaper visited them. Her soon. Brooke carried on. She didn't make it. No one did.

Abby Weston (12)
Barnes Wallis Academy, Tattershall

The Latin Watch

I don't believe in coincidences. What happened on 3/4/30 was certainly no exception. My grandfather gifted me the watch on his deathbed and used his last breath to remind me how important it was to the survival of humanity. Scratched onto the back were Latin words that translated to, 'End of the world'. It had never once started ticking, until the moment the chain of events leading to the sun colliding with Earth began.

I'm recording this in a small notebook found among the ashes. I don't know what's happening. I do know one thing. I'm not afraid.

Kacy Wheildon (13)
Barnes Wallis Academy, Tattershall

The Apocalypse - With A Twist

If your mum told you not to kill the spiders, you may say, "Nonsense, Mum, they're just a nuisance!"

This is the story of a nine-year-old boy called Harvey Brown, but you see, he and his parents were ghosts because the apocalypse had happened early. It happened because of starvation, it was all down to the flies. They'd been allowed to multiply because of the lack of spiders and eat more, more and more of the humans' huge food stock, leaving them starving, and that is how the horrific (yet disgusting) end of the world had happened!

Kerry McDonnell (12)
Barnes Wallis Academy, Tattershall

Robot Revenge

Bang! All the buildings fell. At least half the population died, but the remaining people were really hurt or homeless. It was a cold and wet night, when the two girls, called Brooke and Cerys, realised what was happening in their home town. That night, Brooke and Cerys were getting ready for bed. They heard a big bang! They rushed to the window to see what was going on. Believe it or not, they saw what was happening. Here's what they saw: a dangerous robot pushing a huge rock that was knocking down all buildings. It was coming for them...

Brooke Perkins (12)
Barnes Wallis Academy, Tattershall

Worlds Collide

Bellock tripped, a cliff in front of him, a merciless beast hunting him down. This thing was sure to destroy galaxies. The beast now bearing down on him. He leapt. The wind rushed through his hair and adrenaline pumped through his veins. There was suddenly an oasis five feet deep and he plunged straight into it. He made it to an opening in the cliffs, but this misery was right behind him. He turned around in a heartbeat and whipped out his glowing sceptre, piercing the beast through the heart, blood trickling down its chest, it weakly smiled, but why?

Dylan Hill (12)
Barnes Wallis Academy, Tattershall

Alien Blood

The white mist surrounded the only alien who survived. Was a human hidden? Who knew. Only the story of an apocalypse world may reveal the truth...!

One day, and only on that day, which felt like years back, the truth was revealed. Poppy was an ordinary girl (who was part alien) who lived in a blue sky world named Earth. It was strange and new.

Soon enough, home arrived at the heart of midnight. An alien invasion took place in a house where Poppy lived. Home arrived and they wouldn't stop until they got her back. All human life, gone...

Cassie Clark (13)
Barnes Wallis Academy, Tattershall

A Flaming Catastrophe

Charlie had experienced a catastrophic sight. All around him were ruined wrecks of buildings. He remembered how whirls of fire had just invaded his only home. Screams of horror followed him. Sweat trickled down his throat. Suddenly, a figure emerged! It was a girl. Who was she? She looked petrified and about five years old.

"Who are you?"

"Izzy," she trembled.

"Come on, we have to find somewhere secure," he replied. "We'll look for the others in the morning."

"Fine," she answered. Flashbacks flooded his head. As they found a forest, he wondered, *am I to save the world...?*

Summer Lorna Griffin (11)

Beacon Academy, Cleethorpes

Hope

My heart pounded. "Did that really happen?" Molly said.

"Well, it does look like it," I choked. I looked out the window and saw people panicking. Clouds shadowed my house, the water had risen to the windowsill and now, water was leaking in. We looked at each other in terror.

"What do we do?" she said.

"Leave," I said. "We have to leave."

I opened the window and leapt out, Molly followed. While the rain splashed on my head, waves hit against me.

Three hours later, we found land but not much, and hoped to wake up tomorrow morning.

Isla Stephenson (11)
Beacon Academy, Cleethorpes

Timed Out

End of the world? At first, it seemed completely dramatic, though that would have been different if you understood this catastrophe. You would be just as petrified. This was an apocalyptic heatwave. The worst was the lack of resources. All water boiling, all food turning mouldy, plants set on fire, oxygen slowly disappearing, leaving smoke in its wake. Gas masks? They all melted! There was little survival. All hope was lost. There was no point in survival. No food, no water, temperature rising, no place to go. Nowhere was safe. The end was nigh, for even the strongest.
Time's up.

Ellie-Rose Jasmin Taylor (12)
Beacon Academy, Cleethorpes

1988 Hurricane

"Warning! Breaking news! The deadly hurricane that has already wiped out so many is now heading for Hawaii. Only ten people have survived who were in its brutal path. The catastrophic hurricane has now reigned for over forty-eight hours and we fear that there is no escape with no food. You have water though. *Don't go outside and stay safe.* Hide from this lethal assassin. After forty-eight hours, the horrific hurricane will be over, then you'll be able to move country and live far, far away from Hawaii. You'll be able to have food in forty-eight hours..."

Rhyleigh Priestley (11)
Beacon Academy, Cleethorpes

End Of The World

"Hailee, come on!" Lily shouted, beckoning me to her, but I wasn't stupid. I knew what she was trying to distract me from. The people running, screaming as more wounds mysteriously appeared everywhere on their skin. I looked up and smoke clouded my vision. I started coughing as I inhaled more smoke. I saw red lava spurt out. It was a volcano. All was silent. All was still. There wasn't a single living thing on the planet, except me, but that wouldn't last long, especially with no plants. I started zoning out, staring at the barren, burning land.

Alice Fawcett (11)
Beacon Academy, Cleethorpes

Volcano Of Doom

A serious catastrophe had occurred. A furious, lava-spewing volcano had erupted, leaving thousands dead and many seriously injured. The red, dreaded smoke ascended at 11:27, 18th December 1994 and a few hours later rose another mammoth cloud of fiery smoke, relentlessly spitting furious lava.

Here I am, perilously perched on a large heap of rubble, getting ready to join the many already drowned in the molten magma. As I lie here waiting for it all to end, silence falls.

I sit up and see everything come to a halt. Ash floods over the once peaceful world.

George Allen (12)
Beacon Academy, Cleethorpes

The End Of The World

A worldwide earthquake occurred on Saturday with fatal consequences. The world needed to evacuate as the entire planet was now uninhabitable. Astonishingly, a huge crack appeared through the surface of the planet, causing shockwaves and tremors all over. *I must make it off the planet. I must survive.* I only had enough food to last me a few days and two bottles of water, but luckily, I placed a radio in my bag and heard a broadcast saying to go to a place called the lighthouse. Somewhere east. Let's hope they could help me off this rock. I hoped...

Jayden Lacey (11)
Beacon Academy, Cleethorpes

Outbreak

In 2004, the hurricane was hitting us at 200 miles per hour, the savage wind was damaging everything in sight. It was one of the most intense and catastrophic natural disasters in history. The state was not as it once was. Everyone evacuated (or tried). Some died. Some lived. It had become a post-apocalyptic wasteland. The fear and panic had subsided and now there was just a will to survive.

I killed without guilt. Only the most ruthless survived. I pulled out my eight-inch hunting knife and impaled him. It went through his intestines. It was the end.

Joseph Morton (12)
Beacon Academy, Cleethorpes

Terrifying Tsunami

I was one of the few survivors of the tsunami in Australia. This petrifying wave killed 64,000 people. There were only a few of us left. It started with a rumbling sound, then the Earth started to shake, soon followed by huge, catastrophic waves. The vulnerable islands were now nothing. They were flattened and there were huge cracks in the roads. The deadly sight of this wave made me feel sick to the stomach and I felt automatically trapped. Few people survived and if they did survive, they had been badly injured. I clung to life but hope just faded.

Olivia Carter (12)
Beacon Academy, Cleethorpes

The Heatwave That Changed Humanity

'Dear diary, 29th June 2016: the day the world caught fire. It was boiling hot, flames licked the orange skyline. Warning sirens blasted through the crackling of the ferocious fire. I thought I was doomed but my dad returned, I carried my suitcase with my dog, Dottie, and my friend, Lenny. We left. I looked back, my house exploded with a *bang!* But we couldn't stop now, we just had to carry on. Luckily, we were going on holiday so I'd packed the day before and we had lots of food and water. We didn't starve to death...'

Brooklyn Willoughby (12)
Beacon Academy, Cleethorpes

Holiday Gone Wrong

'Dear Diary, 14th September 2018, I can remember the day of the catastrophic tsunami that killed so many. A pleasant holiday became an unexpected nightmare. The violent wave was enormous... I was petrified. The wave swept me away and I felt like this was the end, but I pushed through it. I climbed to higher ground. It took all I had to pull myself up. My body was broken.

Many hours passed, then suddenly, there was an echoing silence. It had stopped. The apocalyptic storm had finished, but who was left but me...?'

Lucy-Leigh Louise Redfern (11)

Beacon Academy, Cleethorpes

Hurricane

It was just a normal summer's day; people were out walking. Then suddenly, everyone from the beach flooded out from the beach and they were shouting, "Hurricane!" Everyone started to run away like a horde of rhinos barging cars out of the way. A ton of people got caught by the hurricane. 'Dear Diary, it is 2044, I am the only one left in my town. I am struggling to get supplies and I am starving and thirsty. It's a life-or-death situation. Either I give up or keep fighting. I need to decide...'

Harlie Jenkins (11)
Beacon Academy, Cleethorpes

Underestimated Savage

I slammed the door shut behind me. The screams had now echoed into silence but sounds of fatal carnage still haunted me. I covered my ears and wept. My family were out there all alone. My best friend had already been engulfed by the tornado and was gone. A long beep screamed through my body, sending chills all over.

A midnight-black pall covered my vision and I could hear panicked noises saying that I was unfixable. Then my hearing aborted and I was left alone, a black hole sucking me in. The afterlife beckoning.

Jade Bradley (12)
Beacon Academy, Cleethorpes

End Of The World

Was it the end of the world? It had to be. The earthquake shook the helpless Earth and buildings trembled in its quake. Everyone was gripped by fear. I had to escape and take my family with me. Too late - ferocious flames erupted from the ground and swallowed them. Desolation overwhelmed me. All life was gone, but I was saved. Why...? Now, here I was, watching my world, my home destroyed by the darkness all around me. I would never forget that moment. Screams... fear and life. Gone... just gone.

Chloe Freeman (11)
Beacon Academy, Cleethorpes

Earthquake Horror

I remember the earthquake as if it were yesterday. It was something I'd never forget. Rocks were flying to the ground and we were just a few metres from death. I ran for my life, horrified at the sight of squashed bodies. A rock narrowly missed me but destroyed a house in its path. I saw a giant crack form down the middle of the island, heading for me. I jumped to one side.

After, I remember I was being pushed to the edge as the house moved and I jumped over the crack. I had made the jump.

Liberty Scott (12)
Beacon Academy, Cleethorpes

Magma Mayhem

I heard the mountain roar its flames like a breathing dragon. People started to run and scream along the island. "Move to the end of the island!" shouted officers. The mountain of lava slowly spread along the city, burning houses, buildings and people. Myself and James ran towards the end of the island looking for survivors. The magma was still spreading like a tyrant knight. James looked at me with tears dripping down his eyes. "Please, I don't want to die."

I looked and told him to close his eyes. We swam out to sea.

"Where do we go now?"

Muhammad Ali (18)

Franklin College, Grimsby

Humanity's Failure

Australia, 2039. A barren wasteland of sand and dust. The only remains of a once promising future would be the debris and buildings scattered around. There was no time to mourn or to be melancholy, only time to survive. Alex only had a can of out-of-date vegetables, probably well over-boiled from the volatile heat and radiation. The long-lasting effects from the bomb drop, still taking effect years later, corroding everything around. No water, no shelter and no transport. It wouldn't be long before he fell to the ground, succumbing to death: another victim of humanity's failure.

Kira Rose Inkson (17)
Franklin College, Grimsby

Volcanic Eruption

Settling down in my freshly put-up tent, I couldn't bear the burning sensation on my skin from the light touch of scorching ground. Suddenly, I heard mumbling in the distance, getting closer and closer. I was incredibly confused. Two people ran towards me who seemed like a father and his daughter, they looked in shock to see me here. They couldn't stop panicking. Unfortunately, I could not understand due to the foreign language. A sudden explosion made the three of us all stand in shock and concern, we were in incredible danger from the scarring hot magma volcano erupting...

Kinga Japelska (16)
Franklin College, Grimsby

Earthquake In The City

The ground cracked and crumbled as it shook rapidly. The glass shattered with every jolt from the houses surrounding me. The screams were horrifying as they echoed through the air just to tickle my ear as I was stood, frozen, no expression, no feeling. Every second a building would collapse and a mushroom cloud of smoke appeared above it. I didn't know how to help. Cries surrounded me and rubble flew at me like lightning speed. Dust rained down like snow. The orange glow began to get brighter as the building coughed fire. The floor began to break!

Kiera Swain (16)

Franklin College, Grimsby

The End Is Just The Beginning

Over the past week, there had been an object hovering in the sky.

That night, at about 11:03pm, the ground started shaking, buildings collapsing, the noise kept getting louder. I didn't remember anything else. The next thing I knew, I was being dragged out by three people who had a lot of weapons. I looked up and there was nothing, just rubble. It was like the UK got hit by a bomb. We started to walk around to see if there were any more survivors. There weren't. We were alone, or were we? At that moment, everything went dark...

Chloe Johnson (17)
Franklin College, Grimsby

Shake It Out

It started demolishing houses like it wanted nothing left. Everybody was rushing around me, stood there all alone at eleven years old and nobody stopped to help me. The ground had shaken everything until families had been torn apart and until there was no safe place. It hit our home like a bomb, as it had never hit us before. Nobody told me this would happen, the air was full of dust and everybody was trying to avoid being caught up in collapsing houses. It pained everybody to see their homes were mounting to nothing. Nobody ever came to help!

Matilda Jane Bennington-Wiltshire (17)
Franklin College, Grimsby

Will She Survive?

The powerful wind pummelled the sides of the house with force. The house shook, causing memories to fall from the walls. Scarlet sat at the boarded window with a small opening to view the disastrous street. From what Scarlet could see, the water from the river close by was racing down the road. Scarlet was trapped at home, safe - for now - with limited supplies. She could see large, black, thick clouds hovering over town. She felt brave knowing she would survive with what she had left, and safe as she had her loving cat, Fluffy, by her side.

Shannon Louise Austin (16)
Franklin College, Grimsby

Lost Love

As I slumped over her makeshift grave, I sobbed. The trembling ground had resigned, telephone lines sparked wildly, the earthquake had stopped. I saw the ruined cityscape with an orange glow from the burning wreck of the city. I remembered her: my one true love. Now gone. Squashed under a five-ton bit of concrete. I wished I could be with her right now. As the streams of tears ran down my face, I started to lightly sob. I felt a cold sensation on my shoulder and my love giving me the will to move on. Time to face this alone.

Thomas Blow (16)
Franklin College, Grimsby

Live Or Die

People screaming, shouting for their mums: the Earth was falling apart. I saw the cracks appearing in my house walls. It was like a herd of elephants galloping past me as the ground began to shake even more. By then, my house was a pile of trash on the floor as I watched it fall. The taste of dust which approached my mouth was as dry as the floor, I could taste the fear, children running free. It was a horrible sight to look at, knowing everyone would die.

There was a loud scream: then it fell silent. Nothing.

Emelia Petchell (17)

Franklin College, Grimsby

Heatwave

Dragging my feet through the sand that was now lava, the Egyptian sun shone on the desert and burnt me as if I were in an oven. Trembling, I dropped to the floor like a ton of weights and inhaled the last of the bread and water before it deteriorated. Taking a deep breath before looking into the sun's smug face, I dug into the sand. I dug so hard, blisters formed on my once soft skin. Hitting a dense area of sand after what seemed an eternity, I discovered a cooling substance which I could easily indulge in.

Abby Robinson (17)
Franklin College, Grimsby

Death Is Near

I had just woken up when there was a pool of sweat dripping off my covers. This got me wondering what was happening to me. Maybe I'd become strange and developed a rare condition? But no, I was not special at all, there was more going on than met the eye. Well, let me tell you, I looked like a whale that had just died for no reason.

I approached the door with caution, slowly opening it and it hit me. Looking down at the concrete, heat was rising out of the ground, sweat poured from me...

Melanie Jane Sadler (17)
Franklin College, Grimsby

Last Breath Was Goodbye

"Did you hear that?" whispered Lucy.

"What?" Kayler asked,

"It sounded like something got knocked over."

"It's probably the dogs," she guessed.

"They're with Mum."

"Let's both go and see then."

"Okay."

They tiptoed into the living room but instantly regretted it.

"Aaargh!" They knew what the problem was. There was a massive hole. It was an earthquake! Oh no. Kayler began to wobble and so did the ground.

"Aaargh!"

"Kayler!" Lucy shouted. She was hanging by a thread.

"I can't hold on anymore!" Kayler shouted.

"Yes, you can!"

"I love you..."

"Nooo! You can't...!"

Her last breath was, "Goodbye..."

Lucy Radford (11)

Lincoln Castle Academy, Lincoln

Operation: Nightfall

2377. The mould has just been found. Continuing to monitor.

2379. Testing phase initiated.

2380. It seems to alter all it touches. Further study required.

2383. The test tube is thick with black. It grows slowly but constantly. Broadening testing species.

2386. Human testing - ineffective? Transferring to motherland for study.

2402. Subject -7... changed. He's but a viscous liquid. Continuing tests.

2406. "Everyone evacuate! It's sprea-..." Silence. Dormant. Waiting.

2431. It's still spreading. It has consumed all of Iceland. An evacuee has fled to Italy, not knowing what he carries. Venice was lost in minutes. Silent. Dormant. Waiting...

Ryan Homden (13)
Lincoln Castle Academy, Lincoln

The Last Residence

His escape pod had been the only one to launch, everyone else had been engulfed by the detonation of the ship's core. They had been the last hopes of humanity, now it all rested on him. "Good morning, James," had been the pod's greeting to him eleven days after the incident. "How's supplies lookin'?" James had responded, only to find out that he wouldn't survive more than the following days without landing. Eryon-73 was his target, it would sustain his life indefinitely. On the twenty-first day in transit, James landed. Utilising his pod's capabilities, James reformed his life to luxury.

Hayden Edward Smithett (13)

Lincoln Castle Academy, Lincoln

Weathering The Weather

The previous tsunami had hit hard, but didn't come alone! Hurricane George was hitting New York at a speed of approximately 111mph! This could cause mass extinction to all us victims in New York. Yes, unfortunately, we were victims. This was a serious catastrophe as we couldn't evacuate. It would be dangerous. Oh, hang on, I was getting a call.

"Yes, John."

"It seems that the hurricane will be hitting at 3am tomorrow."

"So you're telling me we have fifteen hours to live? John? Hello?"

The connection was gone. Good luck out there, you're alone now. Goodbye, everyone.

Thomas Woods (12)
Lincoln Castle Academy, Lincoln

The Attack

Everything was quiet. *Boom...!* A tremendous noise echoed throughout the shop. The air became hot and thick. There was a strong scent of burning. Suddenly, fire was everywhere. A girl shrieked and ran to her father. Her stuttering body collapsed. She held her ear against his motionless chest. At that moment, everything went still - the screaming and chaos paused. A singular tear crawled out of the corner of her eye. She rested her quivering hand against his cold cheek. "Wake up!" she bawled, shaking the lifeless body. "I need you," she whimpered. *Bang...!*
Once again, everything was quiet.

Rene Fern Brown (13)
Lincoln Castle Academy, Lincoln

World War III

One day, Donald Trump started an argument between China and England. He said something really nasty about China's president so China started World War III against England and started attacking people. This made England's army come out of hiding and start killing China's army. There were twenty-two people protecting China's president but instantly, England murdered them and started running after China's president. Then, when they caught him, they brutalised him until he was bleeding, then they all shot him at the same time.

After, they all went home and started celebrating their win over China in the war.

Alex Fisher (11)

Lincoln Castle Academy, Lincoln

The Fall Of Technology

The year was 3045, over one thousand years after 'it' happened. The 'machines' took over. I know what you're thinking, *it's probably like Terminator or Transformers*. But no. These were like normal, everyday animals except sized up. They didn't even kill for survival or food, it was a game for them or a sport. They were programmed to serve us, to help us, but there were faults in the system, they communicated, they changed. We'd resorted to being cavemen once more. We had to hide, we couldn't fight back. We couldn't kill, not until the 'one' arrived. Not until I arrived...

Reuben Lanchbury Empson (14)

Lincoln Castle Academy, Lincoln

Desolation

The surface of the Earth was barren, lifeless. However, underground lived the last remaining humans. This all happened because aliens had inconspicuously landed on Earth and in remote locations, spanning the entire planet they had taken refuge and had been polluting the air with chlorofluorocarbon. This was most commonly produced somewhere underground as to stay unobserved. To produce and scatter all of that into the atmosphere took a rather long time and the result was devastating; following from that was the total destruction of the ozone layer and the ultraviolet radiation killed every human on the planet's surface.

Nathan Cole (14)

Lincoln Castle Academy, Lincoln

Crumbling Chaos

The eerie surroundings sent chills down my spine. The moon hung innocently in the air. I stood, staring at the ancient, crumbling pillars that created the entrance to the deathly room. Magnificent statues were proudly stood, guarding the place. They were stunning carvings of unearthly creatures, with their wings sprawled out, ready to pounce. As I was fighting my urge to run, everything began to shake. I glared at the stone building, open-mouthed in pure terror. The fiery red candles surrounding the archway flickered, the statues beside began to crack, giving out deafening vibrations, making any living soul quiver...

Lacee Williams (11)
Lincoln Castle Academy, Lincoln

The Gas Elimination

It was a normal day in Wakefield. The Earth was shaking like a freezing child in the winter. Cracks started appearing. It was nothing like an ordinary earthquake. Gas started seeping out of the Earth. People who came across the toxic gas evaporated. When at least twenty-four people evaporated, then we, the citizens, had to take cover. Acid rain, this city was in complete anarchy. Ninety-six percent of the population had been mercilessly snatched. The only survivor was... Seb. He was fighting against Mother Nature. Would he survive this reality that seemed like a nightmare?
Flooding! Civilisation was melting...

Scarlet Rayner (11)
Lincoln Castle Academy, Lincoln

A Burning Desire To Survive

Could it possibly get any worse? Catastrophic events appeared to be quite common within the last year. Scorching, sizzling waves of death advanced. Friends, families, complete strangers - all working together to postpone death. Burning. As lethal as a bullet through a pulsing heart. Courageous, heroic, the police forces fought back. Little could they do other than reach the temporary safety of land further away, saving all they could. Children rounded up like sheep, to escape the hellish magma monster from the volcano. Death was near, lava was here. The volcanic eruption would wipe them out. Could it get worse?

Suzy Miller (13)
Lincoln Castle Academy, Lincoln

Retribution

Cirrus clouds stretched across the sky's frontier, foretelling the hurricane. And the grizzled man walking by the sea wall there, windswept by sands as the deep swell neared, reciting above the waves when the catastrophe lands. A sky-wide judgement in stained rain bonds, the reawakened weather spiralling to where wrath's centrifugal force surrounds a cylinder of wind and ascending air. Where the whipped moisture, whisked by the winds, whistles to the top of the atmosphere - with lifting seas, and blinding sounds - where the witness is both hearer and seer, whirling around the ear, right here and there.

Jayden Griffin (12)
Lincoln Castle Academy, Lincoln

Drowning In Sorrows

Distraught, stressed, horrified after my best friend was burnt to death by the volcanic eruption, the fumes and ashes were suffocating me. Buildings cascaded to the ground. Citizens were screaming due to their loved ones dissolving into lava. The stench of smoke invaded my nostrils. My body was scalded to the bone. I couldn't look any further at my injuries, the thought made my stomach do somersaults. I was determined to find my family and at no cost would I stop scavenging through the islands of thick, warm ashes. I felt someone's hand buried underneath. Was... was it my family?

Lyla Rainford (13)
Lincoln Castle Academy, Lincoln

Science: Gone Wrong!

I was only trying to help! I thought desperately, clutching my open wound. I groaned with pain, my previously white lab coat now stained red, whilst blood was seeping into my shirt. What had I done? Finally, my project was complete. This would be noted down in the history of science! It was... it would change the world! It did... with a flick of a switch, I could stop any natural disaster I wanted! The device was powered on... I couldn't control it. It brought pandemonium, not peace.

Funny, supposedly I was the natural disaster. Now everyone wanted me dead.

Andzelika Grigorjeva (13)

Lincoln Castle Academy, Lincoln

Melt

It was only five years back. Screaming blasts from the eruption. Untameable. Loud shouting filled the room. Buildings remained broken to this day, which was now 2035. Heat rose again, from which heatwaves were visible. *Click!* It was the same exact news report, more serious than before. A beacon of orange liquid light shot into the air. Grasping my phone, I dialled my mother. Reception down. Building shaking. Intense lava flooding the town, the sea now no more than a pile of rocks. We all scattered outside. Buildings collapsed in front of us. Was it over? What...? The melt...

Natasha Poole (13)
Lincoln Castle Academy, Lincoln

Survivors! Be Aware!

Judith Hollows, she's a survivor. Her eyes remember everything.

One year ago she would've had a normal life; would have gone to prom, done homework. She thinks about all the distant memories that were right around the corner from her; like when she would have been cooking with Mum, sunbathing with sisters Jaya and Zila, or choosing cars with Dad, making dens with her brothers or sewing with her nanna, but all she does is run, eat, run and scavenge. Those ravenous monsters are everywhere and keep chasing her. Judith can't get away until she meets a group of people...

Callie-Mai Violet Hind (11)

Lincoln Castle Academy, Lincoln

The True Definition Of Chaos

Chaos, it's a word often exaggerated over problems, after what happened, it's an understatement. No one ever realised we were cattle in *his* plan. And *he* led a bloodied slaughter with his army of dark, deranged beings, unworthy of a title. Destruction began with intense heat spiralling into skeletal monstrosities, tearing through the Earth's crust, with intent to hurt. The few humans remaining hid, most were led to slaughter in the first month.

As of now, it was 2041 and the Earth was polluted beyond repair, for our sins, this was our... punishment.

Deacon Buckthorpe (13)
Lincoln Castle Academy, Lincoln

Rabid

I realised I picked the right moment to leave as I tried to return to make amends, only to discover their mauled corpses, but not from the 'Rabid', but from teeth. Human teeth. Though I would prefer the 'Rabid' with their sport, the slowly-eating cannibals. Lonesome roads are my only option. My group, they were horribly dull and wanted to be supposed 'survivors' but killed innocent people. It seemed their fate caught up.

Earlier this week, a couple opposed me, though I was afraid, I soon realised it was an empty gun and I persuaded them to trade.

Chris Richmond (12)

Lincoln Castle Academy, Lincoln

Holiday Horror

The floors started shaking, we all stood still in worry. *Bang! Crash!* The waves destroyed many, many homes and people's lives. This was a devastating disaster! A tsunami! I couldn't believe my eyes, it overwhelmed me how high the waves were! I had no chance of escaping, this was it for me, I could do nothing! I couldn't help but wonder where my family was and if they were okay, I couldn't bear it! Right in front of me were children screaming to their heart's content, many people would be badly injured or dead. This was a horrific disaster...

Melissa Marie Shears (14)
Lincoln Castle Academy, Lincoln

The Terror Of The Aliens

Glass shattered, people screamed, buildings burnt. The place was destroyed.

Two days passed since the aliens attacked. People thought they left but we didn't think so. Charlotte, Milly and Jackson. We saw them destroy everything and then go into a cave on the outskirts of town. The cave they went into was in the dark, old, dilapidated woods. 152 people dead. 527 injured. It was terrible, blood everywhere.

Me and my friends went to investigate but we were on our own, everyone in the army was dead. We found them in the cave that we very slowly snuck into...

Isabelle Eve Croft (11)

Lincoln Castle Academy, Lincoln

Armegeddon

Dark. Gloom. Void. All I see in my own world. But I'm not alone. This isn't my world. My revolver sleeps in my back pocket as I glare onto the threat, dead ahead. I'm scared here. I want to go home. The hollowing sound of crackling infernos and interdimensional rifts bore me. The old warm welcome and scent of happiness and joy. That's what makes a home. Not the stench of gasoline. The only sound enjoyable is distorted sound through a punished radio underneath rubble from the meteor explosion. Music to my ears. For now, I stay. *Until home comes.*

Harvey Michael Doona-Grummitt (11)

Lincoln Castle Academy, Lincoln

Death Of The Night

Shattering glass, missing children, the falling chandelier, and the smashed portraits. I remembered every touch, every click, every shut of the closed doors. The pain in my stomach deepening by the minute, my anxiety awakening from closed doors. Standing there watching this, this thing destroy my life and loved ones. As I stood, I thought, *I deserved this*. This was my misfortune and this was my death. I kept repeating this in my head, thinking, *what could I have done to make it better?* But it was too late. You don't know about that night, do you?

Kerisha Wahrd (11)
Lincoln Castle Academy, Lincoln

Darkness At The Garage

At the darkness of dawn, all of a sudden, at a garage, there was a vivid black shadow waiting for me. It tried to threaten me by saying, "Wait there, little thing," even though he wasn't moving his lips. So I did, because I didn't want to get injured. He said he was going to kill me. Creatures appeared with his clicking fingers and more of the vivid black shadows came along and kept coming closer. Why was this happening on a dark, stormy night? *Creepy.*

These strange creatures were eerie and they reached out and caught my shaky hand...

Abi Tempest (11)
Lincoln Castle Academy, Lincoln

Dr Dementyev's Diary - Entry 28 - Presumed Dead

It just hit. Ninety-five percent of the world's population wiped out or infected. Cities in anarchy. The military is trying to control it. The only reason I am healthy and alive is because I'm in Siberia, extremely cold and rural. Cold is their weakness. I'm working on a cure involving liquid nitrogen. This will kill them off, and the healthy humans can reproduce in peace. I hope they don't evolve to become immune to the cold. That would be a disaster and we would all go extinct. We wouldn't be able to do anything; the cure wouldn't work...

Krystian Zdrojewski (13)

Lincoln Castle Academy, Lincoln

Drawn To A Close

Finally, I had woken. But to a slightly more pale atmosphere. I glanced outside, and my eyes were rapidly saturated with an image of my street, however, my street looked as though it had been obliterated. A shiver ran down my spine. *What has happened?* I wondered to myself. I instantaneously threw on my clothes and darted out my front door, only to find absolutely no one. I ventured my way across the streets, peering through houses and buildings, observing any forms of life. There was absolutely no one to be found. I had to find out what happened. Now...!

Jack Ashcroft-Day (13)

Lincoln Castle Academy, Lincoln

The Only One Left?

What just happened? A swarm of water came thrashing over me. When I stood up, it covered my hips. I could barely walk. There was no one around, but why? On the news, there was a warning saying a tsunami was striking. I wondered when that would happen. Apparently, it was supposed to happen this morning. Well, I guess newsmen could never be one hundred percent accurate, ha! I figured it ou-

Oh. My. Gosh! Was that t-the tsunami? What if everyone was dead? Would I be the only survivor? What if we couldn't repopulate the world? What would happen...?

Maddison Turrell-Simpson (12)

Lincoln Castle Academy, Lincoln

Is It The End?

We were listening to the news. After that, me and my friend Ambra went into the tent. We heard strange noises coming from outside the tent. *Hrrrr?*
"What is that?" my friend asked. We were scared. Was it the end? My friend and I went outside the tent. There were wolves. Screaming was coming from the way home. We had seen dead people on the floor. Blood was everywhere. It was a catastrophe. Cars were crashing on the streets. The wolves were there. "Help, help!" My friend, Ambra, screamed. No one could help us. Was it the end...?

Daniela Lucan (11)
Lincoln Castle Academy, Lincoln

Run...

As a wave of terror flooded over me, I pelted across to the border; drawing closer with every paw-step. It was chasing me; a swirling vortex of death and destruction. I panted heavily. My pelt bristled as the callous wind hit my whole body. The forest was disappearing; taken away by the monster (or monsters) that were behind me. Leaping over the border, I realised, this was the end. I was surrounded. Everywhere, there was anarchy. My home, gone. Destroyed. Everything I had ever known had been obliterated. My family, murdered. The monsters had destroyed it all.

Bethany Chester (12)
Lincoln Castle Academy, Lincoln

Freezing Drenchers

Her ears gushing with pain, sirens going off wildly had woken her. Perplexed about why the sirens were going off, she fumbled out of bed. A gushing noise arose from outside before she released the door. Droughts had ruled over the land for weeks but now, drenched. Winter was approaching, looming around the corner. The floods kept coming.

Months passed by as the excess water stayed and the weather got colder. Frost began to bury the water. Fractions of the 'lake' began to freeze completely. Soon, the ice tentacles would reach her frostbitten legs.

Isabel Smithett (11)
Lincoln Castle Academy, Lincoln

December 24th

On December 24th, a catastrophe happened in Poland, the north of Poland, and a volcanic eruption occurred. Many people died, with only a few survivors. One of those survivors was me.
On Christmas Eve, me and my family were having dinner, but all of a sudden, we heard a bang... It was the volcano, we needed to evacuate but it caught up with my parents and my brothers. They didn't survive.
The next day, it was Christmas. I couldn't do it anymore and I was missing them like mad! It was time to say goodbye...
"Goodbye Poland...!"

Wiktoria Segiet (12)
Lincoln Castle Academy, Lincoln

The Missing Alpha

One pitch-black night, a girl called Luna went to the outskirts of town and found an abandoned factory. However, strange noises were coming from it, saying, "Luna!"
Her mother found her and told her not to come back.
The next day, she awoke to find she had wolf ears and tail but went downstairs and didn't say anything. She turned on the radio and it said, "There is a pack of wolves on the loose! They said, 'Give us our alpha back. She has a moon and star mark on her left cheek, she's called Luna. Give her back!'"

Faith Croft (13)
Lincoln Castle Academy, Lincoln

It

It was taking over. Controlling more, day by day. It controlled everything they did. Everyone was destroying everything. Glass shattering became familiar to my ears; the smell of blood became familiar to my nose. I felt like I was in a bubble, watching from the sidelines and couldn't do anything about it.

I watched as memories from my childhood disintegrated before my eyes. I had to eliminate it before it eliminated everything. I detested causing violence, but deep down, I knew it was for the best. But they got me. It got me. Now I was a part of it.

Katy Edwards (13)
Lincoln Castle Academy, Lincoln

Nightmare

Darkness. I recalled the blissful days. Everything I once had was gone. Fire... red flames. As red as blood... of... my friends, my family. Burns. They hurt like one thousand needles, but not as much as my loss. I could desperately feel the blood in my veins! Screams... deafening screams! Blood down my neck and hands! What did I do? Darkness came! It was silent. I opened my fatigued eyelids. Light shone on my face. I was miraculously in my bed! Nightmare? No! Yes? I was gasping for air. Frightened. It was...? But then blood dripped from my arms and neck...

Chloe Louise Buckthorp (11)
Lincoln Castle Academy, Lincoln

The War For Water

Ever since the heatwave, it's been a constant fight for water. Fights erupt over a tiny bottle of it. Most of the population died of dehydration but the few who survived went crazy. I got attacked for having a half-empty bottle of water. No one searched for materials anymore. The most valuable thing was water. Me and my group had to fight to survive! It was not just the dehydration that was the problem, it was the sweltering heat that could burn you to a crisp. Mother Nature was punishing us for our constant carbon emissions. She was getting revenge...

Oliver Giovannetti (12)

Lincoln Castle Academy, Lincoln

Behind The Glass

There was a guy with his friends watching a film, they were having a great time eating popcorn, but out of nowhere, there was a bang on the window, but the curtains were closed. Jimmy opened the curtains and saw nothing there. He turned back and said, "There's nothing there."
Everyone screamed, "Jimmy!" He looked behind him. There was a zombie on the window, drooling. Everyone went up to the window and closed the curtains, not knowing what to do. They all locked the front door and then went to the back door and locked it too.

Brandon Thorold (11)
Lincoln Castle Academy, Lincoln

Escape

Just woken up. The last thing I remember was the explosion. We were in the lab testing the chemicals. I was standing at a distance and a blueish blast came out.

I was now in this jungle. The luscious green trees were unrealistic and the fantastic creatures, a bear walked by, not even bothering me, like a squirrel.

I just heard some growling from behind me. I looked and didn't see anything, like something invisible was following me. I turned to look and all I saw was this rabbit with red eyes and sharp teeth, ready to bite... *Help!*

Jake Humphrey (11)
Lincoln Castle Academy, Lincoln

The Choice

So today on the news, we were all shocked to find out a giant meteorite is heading this way and I have a difficult choice to make. Do I send military-grade missiles and hope to destroy it, but it could lead to thousands of tiny rocks heading straight for the Earth, or hope its course will change? I only have eleven minutes before it enters the atmosphere. So my only choice is to blow it up. I must, but it's too risky. Okay, breathe, I've got this, right?
"Seven minutes remaining."
Okay, let's... one, two, three... push!

Charlie White (12)
Lincoln Castle Academy, Lincoln

The Invasion

I could do this. My foot nudged out of the broken canopy. A torch was lying there in the darkness. My anxiety was kicking in! My body slipped out into the cold, wet night. There were dead people everywhere and crushed buildings all around me. As soon as the coast was clear, I ran for it! My mouth thought I was going to be sick! There was a foul stench coming from around the corner. A noise of shuffling, almost munching sounds were heard. Footsteps. Slowly. Heart thudding. They got faster. I stood, still shaking. *Boom, boom...* And then...

Lili-Mai Chardoux (11)
Lincoln Castle Academy, Lincoln

The Last One Alive

I wept. I sobbed. I was phlegmatic. I sprinted through the town in my mind known as memory lane, where I took my first, teeny, tiny toddler toddle across the pavement! What happened, you may ask? Well... I wished upon a star. An incantation I'd set, wanting to be isolated away from the people who hurt me the most. Everyone. More air to share felt like incarceration. I wished everyone away, banished them from my selfish world. I created a catastrophe. One that never had an end. All because of my selfish needs. I was now the last one alive...

Faith Dixon (12)
Lincoln Castle Academy, Lincoln

War

Recently, our lives could have been stopped. We all had lost this everlasting battle. The Germans had taken over the USA. Now London was a mega-target. They dropped some kind of super bomb, wiping out millions. But everyone was saying that we would never give up without a fight.

Here they come. For some reason, they are in incredibly large, mysterious cargo planes or a bomber. It's just flying over France, right now. It's going quicker. The radar cannot keep up. I see Churchill being rushed into a bunker. The bomb, it's here! Help!

Harrison Bower (12)

Lincoln Castle Academy, Lincoln

The Flood

This story began in Saxilby when everything was normal. But then, one day, it got super dry. It lasted for weeks. Gradually, a massive black cloud came above Saxilby. Then, all of a sudden, *boom!* Thousands of tons of water came crashing down on us. I grabbed the closest thing to me, which was a plank of wood. It didn't stop. It kept on coming until the whole Earth was a round ball of water. You know what that means? *Sharks* would be infesting Saxilby. We would be better building boats. I forgot I had a boat. A shark! Aaargh...

Tyler Dalton-Minter (11)
Lincoln Castle Academy, Lincoln

My Dear Daughter

My dearest daughter, my loveable daughter. I can't leave her. The only hope I had, dead! Her cold skin was once warm and full of life. Her once ocean eyes were now cold orbs. Why her? Why not me? Crimson spilt across her skin, the only colour on her now. Back before everything, the world's greatest catastrophe, back then, everyone was happy. Now the tyrant of the world plunged everyone into hell. Starvation, hydration, health. All of it here. Bombs and gunfire. The towering city looking at me. I knew I was all alone in the hell pit.

Justyna Bachowska (13)
Lincoln Castle Academy, Lincoln

Burning Hot

Our skin was burnt red. We were breathing fire.
Shade wasn't available. Our lungs were burning.
Sweating was impossible. Everything had blazed.
Only me, Jack, Archie and Amber were left. The
days repeated: find water and shelter. We were
worn out. The ocean was drying up. Food didn't
grow. We were dying. We should have given up
while we had the choice. It got hotter and hotter
every day. Soon, all the water was gone. How
much longer? Why did it happen? Could we live
any longer? The human race was ending. Goodbye
Earth. Goodbye humankind.

Chanel Parker (12)
Lincoln Castle Academy, Lincoln

The Last Breath

As I ran full out for the bunker, a heavily fortified underground base, there were only a few survivors left in the school. The rest were dead or too injured to move.

The floor around me began to shake. I looked behind and a massive portal opened and out came more of the already invading beasts. I sprinted for safety, having vaporising bullets miss me by millimetres. Just then, I saw it, a fallen alien's gun. I grabbed it and started firing. I dove for cover, then wiped the entire battalion. I made it to the base, it was destroyed...

Morgan James Davis (12)
Lincoln Castle Academy, Lincoln

The Walkers Are Back

I wasn't prepared. Not then, not now, not ever! The walkers are back. One silly mistake had set them off again. This had definitely destroyed humanity forever. I grabbed my guns and tried to contemplate life. Having any hope was pointless. I only had one thing, my baby. Only three months and she would be mine. It was the only thing that stopped me losing my sanity in this zombie-infested world. One day, this would be fixed. One day, I would have a beautiful cottage in the countryside, but for now, I was on my own... fighting for survival.

Chloe Joyce Lowe (14)

Lincoln Castle Academy, Lincoln

Event

When I woke up it was a horrible disaster. I found out that there was only one way to survive it. An unknown, scared girl slammed on my house door because she thought that I should be having breakfast. A few kilometres from my house, people didn't wake up because possibly, they could have died with the flood being outside. It didn't happen a very long time ago, because of the earthquake effect. One million people were killed in the event. The catastrophe was like the end of the world. I was like a great, lucky survivor, wasn't I?

Sophia Cerniaskas (12)
Lincoln Castle Academy, Lincoln

The Day The Sun Burned Out

A soft whistle hummed, cutting the everlasting silence like a knife. None of us had listened. We ignored their warnings for the sake of our pride. Now we cowered, our courage squandered, exactly how we boasted it would never be. Earth was but a fragment, a shard of what it had been. Why didn't we listen? Why didn't we? They said: "Don't bite the hand that feeds you." Then we chewed it off at the wrist with teeth of pride. We were all that was left, broken, damaged. The damn whistle rang like the day the sun burned out.

Grace Walker (14)

Lincoln Castle Academy, Lincoln

The Wind's Direction

The direction, the way of the wind had changed. Looking down at a pitiful village, screams began to erupt. Thanks to the wind. I could hear their cries, even standing upon this cliff. They had called for aid, I'd show them what I'd become. I'd show my father how powerful I was.

I stepped back, only one, then another and another. I'd never felt more alive. Then I ran, to the edge and jumped. And in a flash of lightning, fingers turned to feathers. I was a regal hawk. And I would soar through the sky because I was ready!

Beau Scott-Davies (13)
Lincoln Castle Academy, Lincoln

Horrendous Heat

Severe burns, the scorching ground unable to walk on, I, and only three others had survived. But for how long? We were unable to set foot outside this shop, although not too much heat difference. We were in a large store because it was cooler in there, surprisingly. The heat was so immense we couldn't even walk more than ten metres as we would drain our energy. Then, my friend woke up all of a sudden. He yawned and he breathed fire. It must've been because of all this heat. He never knew that anything could have that much power!

Sophie June Lowe (12)
Lincoln Castle Academy, Lincoln

Kidnapped By Aliens

One morning, I woke up and looked outside and I saw a group of aliens, then I saw the aliens crowding around a house, so I opened my window and said, "Get off my property!" As I knew aliens couldn't speak, but they shouted shut up to me, so I said, "Make me!"

Suddenly, I heard a knock on my door, so I shouted, "Mum, someone's at the door!" So she opened the door.

What happened was that they took my mum away and I was so scared and lonely that my mum wasn't coming back. What will I do?

Aleysha Marie Smith (12)
Lincoln Castle Academy, Lincoln

A Splash Of Disaster

Here I am. Ankle-deep in stone-cold water. I wander the shore like a lost soul as the hot sun begins to beam down on me and the washed-out town. Why, just why didn't anyone believe the warning signs and travel somewhere safe? Safe from all of this.

Alone, I trudge through what used to be a great seaside town looking for any other survivors that lie on the ground before me. I gaze back towards the shore. My heart begins to race. Another huge tidal wave begins to head towards the shore. At that terrifying moment, I run...

Lucy Wright (11)
Lincoln Castle Academy, Lincoln

Avalanche Abomination

I came back from a normal day at school and turned on the radio, packed my things away and heard what the radio had to say. I screamed when I heard the radio say there had been an avalanche and mysterious creatures had emerged from the snow. I called my parents. They appeared and quickly picked up the phone and someone knocked on the door scarily. I quickly opened the door and pointed a knife to their face. It disappeared! Three seconds later, it appeared in front of my mate's house! It had one green face and a blue eye...

Alex Vidas Martinez (12)
Lincoln Castle Academy, Lincoln

The Flooded Submarine

On this yellow submarine, I'm on my own and I'm going five-thousand feet underwater to hopefully find a missing ship in the Bermuda Triangle. We're down a thousand feet right now. Four thousand more to go.

As I'm admiring a ring of different fish, we accidentally go down to ten thousand feet. I make notes. There is a leak in the submarine, it is okay, I'll make it. I gently pull down the lever to bring me back to the surface. The lever is broken. The submarine is full up to the top. The door is stuck...

Charlotte Sophia Ellis (12)

Lincoln Castle Academy, Lincoln

World War Disaster

I headed to North Yorkshire with my squad. It was WW3. After two days, I was in the car. Suddenly, I heard a gun. "Jacub!" I shouted.

After that, my ears became deaf with gunshots. I was shot in the head but my heart was stronger.

I saw a pregnant woman trying to save a child, I grabbed my gun and drew the fire to me. I saw an enemy tank. I pulled the grenade clip and jumped on the tank while saying, "No sacrifice too great, no loss too small!"

I opened the tank and dropped the grenade in...

Kenzie Long (12)
Lincoln Castle Academy, Lincoln

Gas - Our Greatest Fear

Cracks were everywhere. Gas was coming out. The world was ending. Glass was shattering around me and people were screaming. Their screams did not last long as the gas took their lives. It was anarchy. I ran as I tried to find shelter. There was none. People were dying all around me. I felt my lungs trying to reach for air. There were thousands of cracks appearing, swallowing up the corpses. I felt my organs shutting down. I knew my life was coming to an end. The air was too dense. Slowly, I closed my eyes and left this Earth.

Jake Frost (12)
Lincoln Castle Academy, Lincoln

The Heat Is Real

The time has come. A colossal heat cloud has landed on the terrified Earth. The sweat drips from my forehead to the floor. I open the scorching car window but it's no use. The air gets warmer by the second and there is nothing I can do. The air conditioning stops. The car starts moving in an attempt to get somewhere cold. Typically, the car gets low on fuel and overheats. Where can we go? What can we do? My lungs feel like they're on fire. All I can hear are innocent people screeching. It's still getting warmer...

Dylan Lee (12)
Lincoln Castle Academy, Lincoln

Pack Instinct

As I scrambled through the mass of rubble and dead bodies, my ears rang with the sound of falling bombs; my head pounded, my body moaned and I ached with the fear of death. Suddenly, I heard the sound of whimpering. I thought it was just my imagination, however, when I crawled nearer to the source, it seemed more real. Then I saw it. A dog cowering on the severed ground. It looked at me in a meaningful way, then scampered off through the debris. I had an instinct to follow it before it disappeared into the low-hanging mist...

Ella Headland (12)
Lincoln Castle Academy, Lincoln

Their Apocalypse

The epidemic. It ruined my life. I felt my heart pound as I ran away from them. They groaned and grumbled as they got closer. They slaughtered everyone I loved. Everyone said it was going to be fine but it wasn't. I tried to get away from them, brainless, inhuman creatures. I heard the sirens screech. It had only been an hour since it broke out. They always attacked. I didn't dare look back. I lost my breath which led to my demise. They grabbed hold of me. They broke me, tore me apart. I was gone, this time, forever.

Sharn Rhianna Heyward (12)
Lincoln Castle Academy, Lincoln

The World's Demise

The intense heat took us by surprise. My body had transformed into a dark shade of crimson, showing the scars of when the world was put into unbearable burning torture. My once soft hands were now a flakey mess, due to lack of hydration. I picked at the dry, peeling skin every day. I pressed my hot metal can against my dry lips and imagined a cold liquid running down my throat. Suddenly, I felt my legs weaken. Panic bubbled up inside of me as I collapsed onto the ground. My eyes widened in terror as my heart stopped...

Isobel Morrison (13)
Lincoln Castle Academy, Lincoln

The Two Big Bloody Eyes

Hello, my name is Chris and I just turned fifteen years old, but I didn't have a normal birthday. Last Friday, it was the complete opposite! I woke up, I was excited like someone who was just about to win the World Cup! I ran downstairs, hoping to see my parents smiling at me, but no. Nobody was there. So I immediately searched the house. Nobody was in the bathroom or the bedrooms, not in the living room and not even in the garden! I searched the bushes... until I saw big, bloody and grotesque eyes staring right at me!

Freddie Hardy (11)
Lincoln Castle Academy, Lincoln

Risen

Once upon a time, there was a little boy and his dad. The little boy was called Jack and his dad was called Steve. They both were upset because a while ago, Jack's mum died. They were both trying to get some sleep because the next morning, they were going to visit his mum's grave.

At 1:30am they both got woken up by a loud scream. Jack was really scared and he said to his dad, "I heard Mummy downstairs." So they both went downstairs and there was a creepy woman stood up, and it was Jack's mum...

Josh Walster (13)
Lincoln Castle Academy, Lincoln

The Flood

It was the 3rd January 2006, we were all in school. I felt something weird outside. I didn't know what it was. I said, "I saw four people outside, they had black clothes on. I thought they looked a bit mysterious."
School was nearly over and I saw some water coming from the ground. I also looked outside and I saw loads of water on the ground. "Where is that coming from, Miss?" I turned around and saw ten people had been killed on the floor and a person with black clothes on just stood there...

Ruby-Ann Carter (12)
Lincoln Castle Academy, Lincoln

Mission Catastrophe

Today, there is an apparent earthquake going to happen. I know where it is, it's vile. My family know where it's taking place. We also got told to stay away otherwise it would be dangerous and stupid. Well, this sucked! My house got ripped out the ground! I had no choice but to evacuate. We were going to a shelter!

We got to our new home in six months. We didn't have to pay for the house or furniture. I couldn't wait to get a new house!

Five hours later... I was in danger! My life was ruined...

Emily-Jane Abigail Cowdell (11)
Lincoln Castle Academy, Lincoln

Alien Earthquake

"Aaargh! There are aliens!" Peeking out the window with a breath as deep as the sea, my eyes didn't believe what they saw. As one raced towards the window I was at, I looked in one of their eyes and I saw nothing but pure rage! *Kaching!* A small but feisty laser began to melt the ground. The laser sounded like a sword being drawn. Soon after what seemed like an eternity, he stopped, but then... the ground started to shake violently. Was I on a roller coaster?
Then... five simultaneous screams.

Ryan Blanchette (12)
Lincoln Castle Academy, Lincoln

The Flood In Town...

It was Christmas Eve. A flood covered all Lincoln's town. Only me and five other people survived. The houses' insides were flooded. Small children, young ones and elders died. There were only six people left and that was all the humans. We were going extinct. I tried to swim, my skin was getting scales, like the others. Not much food or water left for us all to keep going. Was this the end of the world? Maybe yes, or maybe not.
I was left with a little girl. The end of the world was near and coming for us.

Ambra Bohoslawec (11)
Lincoln Castle Academy, Lincoln

The End Of Lincoln

Here he was, lying on the rotten paths of the hospital. Dave had nothing to live for, every survivor he met tried to viciously kill him. As he left the hospital, he was knee-deep in blood-covered mud. He saw a mysterious figure with a black trench coat, holding a hunting rifle. Dave stepped on a rusty car. This guy wasn't friendly. It was a marine, they were trained to kill since birth. Dave rushed through the doors. He picked up a wheelchair to protect himself. The marine drew his gun. Dave knew it was too late...

Stefan Fota (13)

Lincoln Castle Academy, Lincoln

The Earth Is Shaking

It was a normal Monday until I went to geography. The tables and chairs were shaking. My teacher (Mrs Taylor) told us to duck under the tables. I didn't know what was happening. All I knew was it was terrible.

I saw the cupboard on my friend, I wanted to go help her but my teacher didn't want anyone else getting hurt. But she was my friend and I had to help her. I went up to her, then, *bang!* Another rock fell on her. My face was swelling up with tears. Was that the end of my friend's life...?

Matilda Rainford (11)
Lincoln Castle Academy, Lincoln

Boiling Point

They knew it would happen but they didn't warn us. The human race was shrinking by the second. It felt like a dream; I wished it was a dream. All I could see was the volcanic magma and ash eating the Earth with its presence. Why didn't it take us all? Put us out of our misery? But no. The existence of everyone's peace was now devastation and suffering. Sweat began to drip down my face. I felt like my body was sinking into what was left of the Earth. Why didn't they warn us? They should have warned us.

Scarlet Morris (12)
Lincoln Castle Academy, Lincoln

Worst Holiday Ever

I was going on holiday but the flight was delayed five times and now the sixth time. It was so annoying. I should have left about an hour ago. I hoped nothing bad was happening over there, otherwise, this trip would have to be cancelled, which would be bad.

I finally got on the plane. I would take about four more hours. I had finally arrived. I had to take shelter because a volcano was erupting but not just lava, big balls of molten rock which were very strong. It may be fatal for many people, maybe even me...

Connor Young (12)

Lincoln Castle Academy, Lincoln

The Sunset

I couldn't believe it. They said it was impossible and we were stupid enough to believe them? I knew our planet was damaged, but I had no idea we ruined the one star in our solar system! As a society, we'd somehow managed to take away the one thing that made the world work, that made gravity function properly, that gave us food, energy, and helped us grow. No posters or motivational speeches could help us fix our mistakes now. Eternal darkness, a night without an end, and a black hole, hungry for mankind.

Angel Uzzell (13)
Lincoln Castle Academy, Lincoln

Burning Hope

His skin felt cold yet the air was hotter than lava. As far as I could see, the world around us was burning. My skin was burnt red. It felt like there was fire blazing in my lungs. No matter how hard or how much pain, I held onto him tighter than a koala grasping onto its tree. Caleb was absolutely impavid through these times of anarchy. To be honest, he had recuperated well after his... accident. Caleb scared me sometimes, the way his eyes were as black as onyx when he was lost in the abyss. We're dying...

Maddison Spence (12)
Lincoln Castle Academy, Lincoln

The Last Person

It was another hot day. I was melting in the heat, with nothing to do. I was also running out of water so I had to go outside. I went over to the door and felt the heat hitting my skin - but that was the least of my worries.

As I gazed around in absolute horror, I realised everyone had disappeared, but all the windows and doors were left wide open, nearly off their hinges. Terrified, I saw something alive, green and ugly, lurking around the corner of the house. I was the last person alive and all alone...

John Miller (11)
Lincoln Castle Academy, Lincoln

The Sun Vanished

Over the past few days, I had been getting messages saying: 'Do not let the blue light touch you!' I woke up to utter darkness, I checked my clock to see that it was 10:38am.
Looking out my window, I saw three bright white lights, then I heard a knock on the door. Whoever it was, they continued to knock, so I hid in the basement. I could see a blue light under the door. I suddenly remembered the messages. I needed to hide. I left my torch at the door, reaching for it, the blue light touched me...

Gracie Rose Moore (12)
Lincoln Castle Academy, Lincoln

Darkness

The sun had gone out. Out? You may ask. Yes, it completely lost its flame. Earth plunged into eternal darkness. It was so cold, all the bones in my body were rattling. Me and my family huddled together like a flock of emperor penguins. Teeth chattered as I tried to light a match but it was no use. Frostbite overtook my body like a disease and spread across people like a virus. Humans and all living things were on the brink of extinction as the Earth plunged into the next Ice Age. This was the end of all life.

Olivia Briggs (14)
Lincoln Castle Academy, Lincoln

Tornado Turbulence!

One gloomy night, I was on my luxurious flight home, but then I was awfully surprised by how quickly the night changed... I was starting to drift off when the plane started to circle randomly. I was really confused. At first, I thought it was turbulence, but then I looked outside the window and I was horrified by what I saw. There were trees and cars and I even saw three houses! I started to panic so I immediately jumped up out of my seat and rushed for the emergency slide. I went first. We were in a tornado!

Kaylah Nicholson (12)
Lincoln Castle Academy, Lincoln

How Could This Happen?

It was... I never thought this would happen... It was incredible. I never knew this was real. I thought it was made up. I ran into the kitchen and stabbed myself with a fork (it hurt!). It was real. I was thinking about what to do, should I get my family or not? They may be zombies already! My god! All I could hear was banging on my windows and doors. Help me! Had this really come to an end? How did this happen? The door was opening, there would only be a couple of survivors left. Goodbye friends! Aaargh!

Sophie Hockney (11)
Lincoln Castle Academy, Lincoln

Holiday Horror

It was a normal day. Then the floor started vibrating violently as if a herd of elephants was near. What once was the sound of laughter and fun went silent. Then we saw it. The water. Our worlds filled with panic as people started running. Then it went blurry.

The last thing I remember was the water crashing down on top of me. The next thing I knew, I was on the ground, covered in my own blood. There were dead people everywhere and I was so scared but I was too weak to get help. It was too late.

Amy Madison Sienna Esberger (13)
Lincoln Castle Academy, Lincoln

Survival Skills

Three days since my mother died and I don't know if my food will last me much more than a few days. I need to find a way to kill them, and quick!
I gather all my equipment and create a deadly weapon, enough to kill the leader, the mother. The next day, I find myself crashing through the terrain to stumble upon a nest full of eggs. I wait for around five minutes and good job I waited, as the mother returns. This is my chance. I raise my weapon and throw it at her. It doesn't work!

Charlie Preston (12)
Lincoln Castle Academy, Lincoln

The End

I am in a tree. How did I get here? *Thud!* What is
that? Why is everyone running away? The trees are
falling, what's going on? Is he holding a chainsaw?
There are more, why are they doing this?
Someone needs to stop them and those machine
things. I have to do something. I am going down.
As I go down to see what is going on, a tree comes
falling down. I manage to move out the way just in
time, but then someone with a gun comes up to
me. This may be the end of the orangutan...

Vinnie Pickersgill (12)
Lincoln Castle Academy, Lincoln

The End

It had been going on for many weeks, the volcano just kept getting bigger. People were trying to get far away from the volcano. I had been with my parents at our house all week. The TV didn't work. Everyone had left. There was nowhere to buy food. All of a sudden, the TV turned on and it was breaking news that the volcano was going to destroy the world. When me and my parents heard this, we did not know what to do. So we sat together and waited. It felt like forever. It was the end.

Lewis Smalley (13)
Lincoln Castle Academy, Lincoln

Snowy Education

I am cold! Freezing in fact! Shouting and weeping fills the 'room'. A thick blanket of white snow covers us all! It's so thick and it's getting thicker as more snow falls on top of us. All of us were warm in our classroom until the snow decided to fall from the hill facing our school and break our side of the building! And now, here we all are, covered in the thick, cold snow, not being able to move. I feel like an ice cube or a snowball as snow sets on my head. Why is it us?

Jaydee Millward (13)
Lincoln Castle Academy, Lincoln

Death Is Near

I just wanted to die. I couldn't stand it anymore. The pain. The grief was dreadful. I stood in the middle of the street where I was born, all I could hear was people screaming and crying for help. Dead bodies just lay around me. A woman came up to me and fell apart; her baby had just died from the disease. I wanted to hug her but I didn't. I started to run. The street was so bare. I got to the bridge where I put my son's body. I started screaming and crying. Then I jumped. Why?

Ruby Shaw (12)
Lincoln Castle Academy, Lincoln

Hunt Or Be Hunted

After one harrowing night, morning rose. It was about 7 o'clock. The animals I hunted last night were cooked up for breakfast. As I checked my snares, a wolf was eating one of the rabbits that I caught. I killed the wolf but I only had one snare left, so I checked it and there was a big rabbit in the air. I harvested it and set another snare in both areas.

Out of the corner of my eye, I saw another hunter, so I shot at him to warn him. He shot and the place exploded in an instant.

Alfie Bunn (11)
Lincoln Castle Academy, Lincoln

The Flood Of Africa

It was just a normal Sunday until this happened. I was in my pool, just having fun when my mum heard on the radio that these types of pools were getting too much water and flooding the town. All of a sudden, my pool started to flood. Within five seconds, the outside of my garden was flooded. Me and my mum ran to anywhere we could think of but it was too late. The police had already got anyone that they could see out of there. But what would happen to us? The water was high. Would we die?

Ellie Anderson (12)
Lincoln Castle Academy, Lincoln

The End?

What is this? I thought. I've split from my group. They never wanted me there anyway. They didn't like my train of thought; they were too afraid. They weren't strong, they were scared. So I split from them all and killed them with no remorse. Now I just run. All I do is run and stab. It is a never-ending cycle... until now. I am surrounded. There is no point anymore. They need a meal... They take me away. My arms tingle; the numbness returns. I am one of them now...

Faith Patton (13)
Lincoln Castle Academy, Lincoln

Catastrophe Disaster!

The Chuckle family got in the car and headed out to a place for a family meal. They sat down and waited for their food. The food was ready but the chef put one drop of zombie poison in the dad's food and took it out to the family like everything was okay. They decided they wanted to walk home but the dad started to turn green and crazy. He tried to bite the rest of the family. He started to develop claws like a wolf. The rest of the family tried to get away, but it was too late...

Carly Burnett (12)
Lincoln Castle Academy, Lincoln

Track Your Traces

Here I am in the scariest zombie apocalypse ever. But this is vital, I must know where I'm going and where I've been because life is on the dice. If I mess up here, everything is gone.

Luckily, I find shelter all to myself. I'm fortunate that there's a cold can of meat, besides, it's the most nutritious meal I can have. I hear knocking on the door so I check and there I find most of the zombie race coming towards me. I know my life is over but I try anyway...

Kai Wilmer (11)
Lincoln Castle Academy, Lincoln

The Wonderful World

What has happened to this world? The love, the happiness, all gone. Just me and Death. My family is gone, my friends are gone. The only company I have are the beasts and they try to kill me. I never get to have a break and all I do is run. I can't take it anymore. I walk outside and see the bloodthirsty beasts that ruined this world. We were made to run for sports. I run to live.

I shouldn't be alive, I should be one of them, but I won't stop until they are all dead.

Layton Jay Foley (11)
Lincoln Castle Academy, Lincoln

He's Out There

Climbing up the flaky, red boulders, every step scorching my hands with every touch, but I had to keep going. I got to the top and saw all the chaos. Magma, lava, but worst of all I saw a baby. I jumped across the rooftops to get to him as fast as possible, but would I make it? I ran as fast as I could but fell! There I was, about to be consumed by lava again! But I was determined to save this kid, whether I died or not! I climbed, jumped and tried, but to no avail... Goodbye...

Michael Denman (12)
Lincoln Castle Academy, Lincoln

The Drop

The dreaded earthquake finally hit us, then the disasters started to happen. The floor started to crack. I held onto my sister for dear life as the ceiling started to collapse, running out of our house, we saw it crumble to the ground. Then it fell silent all through the city. The earthquake stopped, but that was not the end of it. It started again, but this time was different, it was stronger than before. Then the floor started to disappear. Panic flooded the city once again.

Courtney Cash (12)
Lincoln Castle Academy, Lincoln

The Eruption

It was devastating. The giant volcano had erupted, with ash clouds filling the air. I was frozen in shock from the boiling lava coming towards me. I was hoping it was all a bad dream. My heart sank in my mouth. I could see the fires of hot lava coming towards me like raindrops going down a drain. I could hear people screaming whilst the lava ended their lives. The taste of fright filled my mouth to the point where it was unbearable. There were no words to describe this.

Charlie Smith (12)
Lincoln Castle Academy, Lincoln

The Earthquake

In 2024, Friday, April 22nd, in Monserrat was a very calm place. All of a sudden, a seismic earthquake triggered a really bad signal. They were going to tell the city there was going to be the biggest earthquake in history about to happen. The city split in half, quarters and more. Justin and Hannah were stuck. They had nowhere to go and all of the seismic earthquake monitors blew up from how strong it was. They both tugged and cried because the city was getting shredded.

Morgan Higson (11)
Lincoln Castle Academy, Lincoln

The Volcano Eruption

Ryuk was running as fast as he could to get away from the volcano. He could smell the smoke behind him, chasing him. His face was already pale but his face (due to expecting to die) got more pale by the second. He saw a car with someone in it behind him. He went to get in, then stopped when it got swallowed by lava. He was too slow and he knew he was too slow and he stopped from a loss of hope, but then he got caught and was still perfectly fine! That's very odd!

Oliver Jamieson (11)
Lincoln Castle Academy, Lincoln

Love On Fire

Hi, I'm Nekoet and this is the story of how I learnt to control my powers... When I was a baby my parents died in a fire... When I was twelve, I met Dmitri. He was my only ever friend. He and I grew closer, but one day, my magic grew out of control and I blasted him with a fireball... Suddenly, there was a spark of pink and a heart formed above us. He kissed me and told me he loved me and that is how love saved me and I learnt to control all of my magic powers.

Charley Burton (12)
Lincoln Castle Academy, Lincoln

The Heat From Yesterday

My face was full of heat. Scorching heat, sweat dripping down my face; I had no hope for my future life. My once beautiful skin, now covered in peeling, flaky, red blisters. The deathly shrieks of my family still haunted me. Three of us survived, not knowing who these strangers were, lonely as this heatwave hit me. It must have been five days since it happened. How was I meant to survive any longer? I feared for what was yet to come...

Freya Annaise Parkinson (13)
Lincoln Castle Academy, Lincoln

Risk It

Once upon a time, there lived a teenager called Billy. He had always had a passion for surfboarding. His grandpa was a professional and then retired at fifty years and for Billy's birthday, he bought him a surfboard and then took him to the beach to try it out. They went out to sea. Then Billy bellowed, "Look at that big wave!" But it was no ordinary wave. It was a tsunami...!

Addison James Hopkins (11)
Lincoln Castle Academy, Lincoln

Turned Cities

I was running and all the zombies were behind me. I gasped. They had lots of breath. I hid around the corner. They passed. I went around the corner. I stepped on a twig. They heard it. I ran as fast as I could. It was tiring so I shot most of them, but they didn't get hurt and they caught up...

Tylor Jones (11)
Lincoln Castle Academy, Lincoln

Last Chance

"Uncle?"

"Yes, sweetheart?"

"Uncle, where is everyone?"

"... There is something I must explain now, my young niece... It all happened so suddenly, the world was getting hotter, but not like America. Then, one day it was so overwhelming, skin melted, houses collapsed and sand became glass. No one survived. Across the planet, the ground shook at magnitude ten, tornadoes whipped up skyscrapers, lightning scorched everything mankind stood for, tsunamis drowned all that remained. Britain was far away from all but storms, so the only known survivors were here, and here we stayed till God's wrath passed away, trying to rebuild civilisation."

Samuel Bowring (13)

St George's Academy - Ruskington Campus, Sleaford

Virtual Reality

I never thought that's how the world would end. Hurricanes. Tsunamis. Volcanoes... Complete destruction...

Five years later, I still can't rid my head of the nightmare I found out that day. We were merely characters in a game played by aliens in another dimension wearing virtual reality headsets. Our world ending - just another level to them.

21st October 2034, earthquakes hit day after day. Volcanoes coughed out millions of tons of magma; scorching the Earth. Then... darkness... No electricity. No Internet. A deathly silence. A final effort. Meteorites rained down. Millions dead... Survivors reached level two... would we survive?

Charlotte Burton (12)

St George's Academy - Ruskington Campus, Sleaford

Pressure

Crack! The Earth started to shake rapidly. Everything was shaking and falling everywhere. Part of the city destroyed, buildings falling apart, families being ruined. All caused by the government's choices. It was their fault. They made the wrong decision. The clouds hovered, showering everyone with rubble from parts of buildings. Strikes of electricity struck from the sky. The Earth was red-hot like magma. Volcanic bombs dropped from the sky. The centre of the Earth, the hottest part. All of a sudden, the middle went up in flames. All the buildings shot up into the sky and exploded everywhere. *Boom! Bang!*

Libby Gardner (13)
St George's Academy - Ruskington Campus, Sleaford

Broken-Hearted Bomb

Implanting a bomb is a power. The world is a power, a bomb, shattered into fragmentations and located under every country. One source is still ticking slowly, enduringly, waiting for its moment to percuss and put the Earth into agglomeration. Spending an exquisite vacation in Italy wouldn't seem defective until you unexpectedly ascertain that you're the last country left which is about to combust. Of course, it's a ghost of a chance but six strangers have to compromise. Life is a big uncertainty. These six take it. They initiate, exploit and will be commemorated if... three... two... one... *destroy.*

Louise Hirst (12)

St George's Academy - Ruskington Campus, Sleaford

I Am Jackson

Once a person's infected, it's only a matter of time.
I walk across the polluted streets of London,
watching the remnants of humanity twitching,
violent spasms extinguishing their last traces of
life. Fearfully, I pick my way through, stopping only
to drink from the puddles of water that remain
from the last treacherous storm. With food spoiling
rapidly, the corpses may soon be my only
sustenance; leaving may be my only hope, perhaps
out there, I might find safety.
Packs of feral hounds prowl menacingly towards
me. How quickly they've changed. Before the
plague, they were pets, just like me...

Hannah Hicks (13)
St George's Academy - Ruskington Campus, Sleaford

The Wrath Of The Ancients

Today begins the wrath of the ancients, sparks will flare in the sky, mixing vibrant colours with evening sky. Tides will turn and Earth will cry as its sky will fragment. Seeping magma from the core will slither through the crust, releasing its bloodlust, decimating life. The scourge of the corrupter will splinter the moons, the shattered debris befalling the Earth. Forests will ignite with a raging flame from radiated heat expelled from nearby implosions. Maelstroms will open the azure oceans and nebulae will barricade the Earth from the cataclysmic events in the astral sky. The calamity will momentarily begin.

Joseph Dean Miles Enderby (13)

St George's Academy - Ruskington Campus, Sleaford

Kansas Disasters

Josh was an ordinary teenager, he was currently travelling to Kansas for a school camping trip. As he arrived in Kansas, a huge outrage was happening, a sudden news report took over the radio which had an alert not to drink the water from any resource. Josh thought to himself, *at least I have enough water.*

Sirens grew louder and louder as cop cars, fire trucks and paramedics sped past.

Many hours later, Josh arrived at a small motel. He heard an explosion which caused an even worse commotion. Nearby, a chemical factory exploded, shattering into millions of pieces...

Gracie-Leigh Jaggs (12)

St George's Academy - Ruskington Campus, Sleaford

The Day Of The Z

They shamble across the streets we once stood in, infecting anyone who dares to come near them. Their faces, a mangled recreation of what they used to be. The government sends air strikes, trying to eliminate the infection, not knowing it'll just spread further, the dead becoming reanimated into the horrors themselves.

An evacuation zone is set up, only to be stormed the following day. All it takes for the virus to begin is a strain of mutated rabies with no cure. There wasn't even enough time to make one.

I'm Shaun Stevenson and I will survive the Naracala virus.

Joseph Swann (13)

St George's Academy - Ruskington Campus, Sleaford

Bombs Away!

The year is 2020 and there are only two people left on the Earth, Noah and Mandy. These people have been trying all their lives to make the world a better place, so God left these people to rebuild civilisation, he had given up on the rest.

Mandy and Noah awoke in a semi-destroyed building with a note describing their mission. They walked outside to see dead bodies, blood, rubble and leftover bombs. Mandy fell to the ground in despair. They shouted to find other survivors but only silence remained.

Then suddenly, they heard a *tick, tick, tick... Boom!*

Olivia Rice (12)

St George's Academy - Ruskington Campus, Sleaford

Fire! Bombs! Decisions!

Fire, bombs, decisions; all is yet to come! A day like any other, for no one knew their lungs would end up empty of life. Everyone went about their day; until the unthinkable happened. The explosion could be both seen and heard from the opposite side of the world. Both Jayla and Jasmine, two girls who had never met, would soon fight to keep the world alive. As though driven by shuddering emotions, an uncomfortable premonition of fear pivoted their senses. A bomb, a bomb... and everyone was gone. Blinking sweat from their eyes, they wondered... What would happen next?

Natalie Louise Howard (12)

St George's Academy - Ruskington Campus, Sleaford

The Falls Of Death

As the unexpected volcanoes started rising from the ground, lava started spewing from the tops. Emily screamed my name to try to make me run, but I was dazed, I couldn't move. I was stuck. Emily screamed my name again and I was brought back to Earth. "Quick, over here!" she screamed. I followed, shaking, as I ran. When all of a sudden, the ground started shaking so violently that most people surrounding me were thrown off their feet. As I tried to stand on my feet, the ground started shaking. A crack came through the Earth, Emily was gone!

Libby Curtis (11)

St George's Academy - Ruskington Campus, Sleaford

The Day The World Ended

It was the 20th of July, the world was ending, these days were seeming a little strange... That day, a bomb had been dropped, letting out a contagious virus. Suddenly, the impossible happened. The ground started to shake around me. There was no escape! All I saw were police officers and people trying to clamber to safety, yet it was impossible. Then I heard the sound of sirens in my ears, wherever I looked there were ambulances, people being taken away, dead or alive? Standing in the middle of the road; the village was a ghost town... *Fire!*

Grace Emily Hands (11)
St George's Academy - Ruskington Campus, Sleaford

Cluster Of Mayhem!

Horrifying storms and asteroids bombarding the planet caused earthquakes, forcing volcanoes to form all across the globe! Furthermore, scalding and deadly wildfires spread to ruin most vegetation. For now, food was a trace. It seemed Planet Earth may be on its last legs.

I woke up in a dark structure to find that it was still night. I went outside to see asteroids crashing down and a dim glow of fire all around me. Trees turned to ash. I heard huge thunderstorms heading my way.

All of a sudden, the ground shook. I looked up to see...

Ben Bunting (12)

St George's Academy - Ruskington Campus, Sleaford

The Broken

19th March 2029. London had been completely destroyed. It was only me left, fighting for survival as I walked through the cold-blooded streets, keeping a peeled eye on every corner, expecting anything to jump at me. As I walked around the corner heading onto Down Street, I had my freshly sharp blade grasped in my hands. I looked across the road and saw a crawler, if you go anywhere near this awful plant, it will sting you and you will have blue, purpley veins running through your skin and die a slow, painful death. Would you be able to live?

Jacob Doughty (12)
St George's Academy - Ruskington Campus, Sleaford

The End Of The World

God was dead and so was the world! Only three remained: Jayla, Lily and Stella. Their hideout was destroyed by an explosion. No one knew who or what caused the issue, however, everyone knew to hide. As the three girls walked down the street, the sound of creaking filled the air around them. The top of a building fell on top of Stella! They had to leave her.

Just then, a ball of fire plummetted down to the ground. Thinking Lily would help her, Jayla went to her. Suddenly, Lily pushed her! But she lived... Jayla was the new God!

Chloe Hargreaves (12)
St George's Academy - Ruskington Campus, Sleaford

The Storm

As the palm trees viciously swayed in the angry supercell, I felt the mysterious Earth go quiet as the wind picked up and the rain fell down rapidly. A mesocyclone formed as a vortex began to swirl and gather all its anger and prepare to burst and destroy anything in its way. I saw it get bigger as a rush of fear travelled down my spine and reached my toes. The grey clouds watched the people down below get sucked into the vicious tornado created. I wanted to know: where was my mum? What was she thinking? Was it goodbye?

Abigail McMunn (12)
St George's Academy - Ruskington Campus, Sleaford

Hell

When I looked outside, all I could see was toxic ash flying through the sky. Nothing to be heard but the flames. I walked around to see if anyone was there, but there was just no sound. The whole world went up in flames, everything just became dry. No water, no rain. Just drylands, well-burnt grounds. I walked to a couple of houses and heard a sound, someone was trapped under something. I ran towards the house and shouted if anyone was there, but it was too late for me to help. I guess I was alone forever.

Joshua Lee Young (15)
St George's Academy - Ruskington Campus, Sleaford

A Warm Welcome

It started when I was taking a cab down Main Street past the giant space needle when the warm, sunny sky turned to a devastating grey. The wind was blowing towards the storm, causing papers and magazines to fly everywhere. My cab and the other cars on the road screeched to a halt, the engines were fried! Then out of nowhere, lightning struck on the gigantic tower and blew the whole thing up! Everyone ran out of the area! My driver ran and left the locks on. I tried to break to freedom. Then I saw it...

Rhys Davies (11)
St George's Academy - Ruskington Campus, Sleaford

Deleted!

We all knew this was the end! The end of all living and the end of all humanity. Just one press of the button and we would be gone in the blink of an eye. It wasn't our fault, bad and evil took over Planet Earth.

Now, God was going to kill all humans and all his creations. We weren't the only ones who would die. However, one press and two would die. We didn't know who else would die and we never would.

All went quiet. My name was Edward Shillmore and I live on Planet Earth!

Kayleigh Abigail Holly Voase (12)
St George's Academy - Ruskington Campus, Sleaford

Hurricane

Only just a few moments ago was I laughing and smiling. Now the world around me was destroyed. No signs of life anymore. The wind pushed down against my body, it was holding me down on the hard stone floor. Panic rushed through me, was this really what was happening? The mist of destruction circled around me, debris clattered to the ground surrounding me. For a moment, the devastation had sunk in, I wouldn't be able to survive for much longer. The blood began to pour from my wounds. I felt my body fading away into nothing. I was scared.

Amy Wilkes (12)
The Priory City Of Lincoln Academy, Lincoln

A Sudden Eruption

The volcano rumbles. Thick, burning red lava falls down like rain in a storm. Screams of panic invade the air. Silence. Hot blisters tear through my skin like a chainsaw. Ashes fall on my tongue, the taste fills my throat. We run for our lives, knowing we probably don't have long left. I feel the heat burning my back. As we start to accept the end is near, a swarm of helicopters come to our rescue, like guardian angels. The ladder drops. I sprint for my life but trip. As I lie on the ground, the lava slowly gets closer...

Eloise Hall (12)
The Priory City Of Lincoln Academy, Lincoln

Boiled

Me and Abby were just sat on the beach when the sand underneath us started burning our skin. Seagulls started dropping from the sky onto the sand and into the ocean. We both jumped up at the same time because our skin was blistering from the intensity of the heat. The ocean looked crisp and cool so we both ran to it, trying to avoid contact with the sand as much as possible. When we dove in, the water started bubbling all around us. There was no escape from the scorching heat. We were going to die. It was over.

Faith Parker (12)
The Priory City Of Lincoln Academy, Lincoln

The Horrendous Heatwave

Wow, we are going through a massive heatwave that is supposed to kill a lot of people and it is going to happen for a few weeks, so you will be extremely lucky to survive, and I mean extremely lucky. So far it has been four days and millions of people have died. They are melting like ice cubes. If you'd like to have a chance at surviving, stay hydrated, wear suncream and stay in shaded areas at most times. We are now nineteen days into it and humanity is close to extinction. Who's next? Will it be you?

Kayleigh Clavin (12)

The Priory City Of Lincoln Academy, Lincoln

Heat

There's a heatwave. I'm alone in the woods, struggling to breathe in this appalling heat! I need water. I need this heat to disappear. I need help. Is there anyone left? This heat burns me inside and out. I don't know how long I can take it. All I have is water, a torch, a backpack, a med kit and clothes. I wonder if I am the last man standing. I need to find a way out of this heat. Everything around me is burning to the ground. I'm going to die out here. Let's act fast now, help!

Lewis Meekings (12)

The Priory City Of Lincoln Academy, Lincoln

Mysterious Box

She grabbed me, shoving me under a waterfall and scrubbed me with a giant brush. The woman took a sharp knife and dug it deep into my skin, making a cross, putting a thick chunk of god knows what into my wounds. I was left for all of five minutes before I was put on a large, cold circle and into a box. A black box, much more immense than I had ever seen. I heard a loud noise. Suddenly, the heat rose and my skin felt ablaze. My head suddenly burst. I was going to die! I screamed loudly.

Katie Founds (12)

The Priory City Of Lincoln Academy, Lincoln

Swallow Me Whole

The sun blazes against my bare skin, gouging through with unbearable sensations. Blossom trees shower me with their delicate, baby-pink petals, hiding me from the bright sky. My school backpack rubs against my torn shoulders, blistering skin turns red-raw. Suddenly, Japan's finest ground starts to shake vigorously, knocking me off my feet, plunging down. Screams of terror ricochet off buildings crashing down into deadly dust. Mysteriously, vision comes springing back to life, the home I used to know has viciously turned into black and dust. Surrounded by vibrating faults, the only option is to jump into the Earth's fiery core...

Mya McVeigh-Judd (12)
Winterton Community Academy, Winterton

The Ring Of Fire

The heat was incessant, it never stopped. The lava kept on coming, swallowing everything in its path. The Pacific transformed into an ocean of steam. It was unbearable, my microphone was hardly working! The lava droplets were cascading from the sky like rain covered in blood. People behind, screaming in disbelief, "You're dying, you're dying!" Everyone was panicking. Men, women and children were running, trying to dodge the flow of the scorching lava as it flowed downwards like rapid rivers into the Pacific.

Two hours passed, still no sign of it stopping. Would it ever stop...? We would never know...

Ellie Crampton-Pullan (12)

Winterton Community Academy, Winterton

Survival Of The Hottest

Running faster than the speed of light. Screaming everywhere around me. My heart was pounding. I could barely breathe. There it was in front of me... *the volcano!*

"Danielle, look at this. What are we going to do?" I shouted.

"I have no idea. We have to help!"

Then I heard it rumbling, roaring, ready to erupt. *Think!* The mountain. It was the furthest thing away from the volcano. How would we get everyone there? *The train!*

Five minutes later, they were on. From the volcano, rocks flew around us. Danielle was hanging off the edge, grabbing onto my arm!

Harriett Hall (11)
Winterton Community Academy, Winterton

I-Fall Tower

Fire... Screams... Bangs... All of these noises echo in my ears. I need to run. Suddenly, I stop as I see the criminals behind all this. Where's a good policeman when you need him? While *frozen* in fear, I manage to blink, then at that moment, they're gone...

After I realise where I am... *Creak!* Looking behind me, there it is. The Eiffel Tower. The big piece of scorched metal stands before me. Bigger and bigger cracks form, creating louder and louder creaks. The last thing I see is... "Mum?"

Within seconds, flashbacks of memories fill my eyes... then, black.

Keira Ramseyer (12)
Winterton Community Academy, Winterton

The Heat Will Rise

The ground submerged in lava, rocks as scorching as stepping stones, the sky was a blanket of ash shadowing the planet. Many people vanished into the depths of the unknown. Lying below the sea of unbearable-to-touch lava, lay the once devoted streets of the humble city. Few people left, the brave survivors on the remaining safe spots. On top of roofs on weak mountains, the heat quickly rising inches each day. The sky began to fill with developing rain clouds, blocking the planet's light. The bitter raindrops racing, pounding on the lava. Concrete struck across the distance. What now?

Lanny Barton (14)

Winterton Community Academy, Winterton

The Mighty Disaster!

The news came on the TV in the morning, a worried-looking reporter gravely delivered a warning for a flood in Cleethorpes.

A few hours later, the afternoon news was on BBC. 'Breaking news! Breaking news!' The message flashed in a red alarm. The flood was the biggest one in the world. 'New update!'

People were dying by drowning. There were people screaming and shouting around, so scuba divers came down with their jet skis so they could be rescued safely. People were rushed to hospital in a convoy of wailing blue lights. Would they rebuild the mighty Cleethorpes?

Curtis Bailey (13)
Winterton Community Academy, Winterton

Ferocious Flood

One thousand years in the future, on Planet Ganshorr, an acid plant caused a terrible disaster, flooding a village with toxic acid! People were stranded in houses, schools and even boats! At just a touch, the acid would deteriorate flesh in a second!

James was at home when he felt a burning feeling in his foot. He gazed down, his bed was melting, his foot had disappeared. He was in excruciating pain! His brother was the other side, crying for help. "Stay strong brother," screamed James.

"I love you James!" cried his brother. Was it too late to save them?

Dylan Walker (13)
Winterton Community Academy, Winterton

Pompeii Relived

We'd been warned about this type of thing before and so far, nothing had ever happened. Therefore, when all our neighbours, friends and family evacuated, we still weren't worked up about it. My mum and dad had contemplated evacuating but after all the false alarms, they expected another one. However, we woke up the next morning to see lava travelling expeditiously down the streets, taking everything in its way with it. Before we knew it, our car was swallowed up by the scorching red lava. Immediately, me and my brother ran to wake up my parents. "Help us! Now!"

Erin Taylor (12)
Winterton Community Academy, Winterton

Ash And Flame

Deep within the Earth's core, a war was raging. Plates the size of entire continents ground against each other in a silent scream of agony, suppressed under rock and ash. Flame licked and curled, waiting for its call for battle. Far above, the maniacal grin had prised through the fortifications of ancient rock. The drums of war echoed out of the ancient mountain.

Liquid rock erupted from the mouth, forced against its will to cast death and misery onto the land of the innocent. Creeping down the rock, flame hissed and lashed, killing those amongst its path.

Andrew Carter (15)

Winterton Community Academy, Winterton

The Rage Of The Rippers!

It all started four years ago when the first heatwave happened, wiping out half of New York and bringing terrors with it: Rippers (zombie-like creatures). The night always brings new, fearful monsters, some leave behind devastating destruction. To the current day, the city is covered in sand and dust; one team of heroes remain - TUDF. The Ultimate Defence Force. They rescue the stranded, or they try their hardest to. With only five in the gang, and Oliver, a teen, as their leader, they must do what they can to survive until help comes. That's if it ever does...

Oliver High (11)
Winterton Community Academy, Winterton

Going Up In Flames

What a beautiful morning it was in Indonesia! The glowing sun was already appearing behind a clump of candyfloss in the sky, it flickered like flames dancing as they burnt. On the horizon, stood Mount Merapi, an active volcano. My parents had decided we were visiting the usual Sunday market just down the road. We reached the deserted market town, not a single soul stood there.

Suddenly, the ghost town silence was broken by the explosion of scorching lava from Merapi's mouth. Tears rolled down my face, fearing death. For the first time ever, I cried...

Maisie Lamingman (12)
Winterton Community Academy, Winterton

The Earthquake!

It was the 13th of November. I was asleep so soundly, no bother. All of a sudden, a massive shake woke me up. Then screaming, shouting and bawling broke the night's silence. I had no idea what was going on. Another shake! The roof was collapsing inwards! I ran as tears streamed down my cheeks, running to my mother and father to see if they were okay. They weren't there. I looked outside. They weren't there. Another shake! The walls started crumbling while I tried to get out. Where was the door? Another shake! The house collapsed... Was I safe...?

Erin Gerry (13)
Winterton Community Academy, Winterton

Splitting The World

The year 1837. A massive earthquake shook the world. Mary could feel the gargantuan tremors: she started packing her bag. Mary was running around the house crying because she had never felt an earthquake this overpowering. She went outside and she couldn't see anyone: she was all alone. Mary found a rope and pulled it... *The world split apart.*

Mary looked down and all she could see was the modern, new world below her feet... but there was lava... Mary threw down the rope and attached it to a tree. She lost her balance and down she went.

Anya Lynne Wright (14)

Winterton Community Academy, Winterton

Will She Survive?

Late at night, a little girl called Emily was going to bed. She and her dad were really upset as Emily's mother had died a year ago that night.

The next morning, Emily woke up to a very loud village. Everyone was screaming, shouting and people were even shooting guns. Emily didn't know what to do as she was only five years old... Emily went outside to see what was happening, she saw cracks in the floor and buildings falling all over the place. She started to hug her doll and started screaming for help. Emily looked up and *boom...!*

Robyn Angel Byrne (11)
Winterton Community Academy, Winterton

Help Or Run, The Volcano Is Round The Corner!

Adam Chambers grew up in a good neighbourhood in Iceland; there was always a risk that the active volcano they lived near could erupt! But then... a rumble through the ground; the air sirens went off. *The volcano erupted!* Adam and his dad helped the elders and other families get out of town and the fire brigade, police and ambulance came rushing to evacuate. Adam and his dad got thanks from the emergency services.

After they helped all the people got out of town, it was their turn to leave... they were out of gas! What happened now then?

Damon Corney (13)
Winterton Community Academy, Winterton

Crumbling World

My baby shrieked and bawled as the moans and low growls of Mount Vesuvius bounced inside the walls of my head. I was going into override. People charged across the streets, the wine shop's shutters closed, almost prepared for the restless and dominant monster of this land. Little did we all know it was too late. Far too late.

I looked down to the only thing I had left, held in my arms. Such sweet eye contact with my boy, my world. Our bond strong, our hearts close... "I love you, I really do," I whispered. Goodbye, my sweet boy.

Eve Ellie-Mai Gurbutt (14)
Winterton Community Academy, Winterton

The Unexpected

I was asleep when I heard my sister Maisie scream, "Help!" as half of the hotel fell to the floor like a waterfall. I picked Maisie up and ran. I ran for my life down the spiral stairs. I couldn't see, dust was everywhere. I looked out a broken window and realised it was an earthquake. I felt a crack underneath my feet. I started falling. I held my sister so tight so she couldn't fall. We hit the floor. I thought I wouldn't make it. I looked at my sister, worriedly, she wasn't breathing. I realised she was dead.

Lauryn Walker (13)
Winterton Community Academy, Winterton

Shaken!

It was midnight when it happened. Toby barked a warning, but no one else understood, just me. Seconds after his alert, the ground shook fiercely. I leapt out of bed but the Earth shook as I did so. Scrambling to my feet, Toby ran to the door, telling me to leave. Obeying his orders, I scooped him up and left. Staring up at the house from the dirty concrete, Toby, unsettled, whined sadly. The ground shook again and cracked, all around him. I screamed loudly as he fell... I thought he was gone... but I couldn't have been more wrong...

Martha Isabella Moon Walker (11)

Winterton Community Academy, Winterton

Living Hell

It has just started. The living hell, we want it to end but it has only just started. The floor breaking away, debris and dead bodies everywhere. I scream for someone to help me but no reply. "Is anyone out there?" I want someone to reply but I know there will be no one. I clean the deep cut on my arm and put a bandage on and continue searching.

"Dr Shawn Brown! Help me!" I hear a random shriek, it's as loud as a trumpet. I run towards the shriek but the floor suddenly drops from underneath me...

Cerys Webber (14)
Winterton Community Academy, Winterton

Dead!

It was the night of the 25th when Lily and Sophia Gardener woke to an enormous bang that shook their beds. Lily hopped out of bed to peer outside the window. Outside was a humongous river of lava. The debris of the village was floating in the street. She turned around and Sophia was gone. Lily ran to find her but running underneath the door was a steaming pool of lava.

Suddenly, the door opened and revealed a dead Sophia. It was time. She opened the window and soared into the night sky. Below, dead, was her mum and dad.

Summer Rush (11)
Winterton Community Academy, Winterton

Crumbling

I was running from my house quickly, as fast as I could. As I looked back, objects were flying off from table surfaces and flying to the muddy ground. We had no time to protect ourselves from the incoming danger ahead of us, so we were all covered in many deep cuts and bruises. It was a nightmare. As soon as I had escaped from the danger inside, I saw everyone running and screaming. It wasn't long until I heard my parents scream, *"Get out of the way!* That was when I realised the house was crumbling down.

Phoebe Swann (13)
Winterton Community Academy, Winterton

The Never-Ending

It's been two years since the hurricanes hit this Earth. Human civilisation as we know it will never be the same, as people fight for survival, I am faced with protecting my family from the dangers of the world. My name is Daniel Edwards and this is my story.

Day by day, I wonder if this world will ever be the same, hoping my children will be able to live their lives in peace. But I know deep down I'm their only hope. I'm the only one who will protect them. If you find this, keep your loved ones close.

Jake Walkenden (14)
Winterton Community Academy, Winterton

The Heatwave

During the summer of 2018, areas around North Lincolnshire experienced their hottest heatwave. This was a time no one would forget. It was exhausting and tiring and everyone was fearing the worst. Me and my friends, family, were sweating like water dripping out of a fountain. Me and my sister were making dens to shelter from the scorching heat. Suddenly, a cloud came hovering across and we all breathed a sigh of relief. We were happy. Was it going to rain? Or was it going to thunder and lightning like never before?

Tristan Robinson-Marriott (12)
Winterton Community Academy, Winterton

Three Minutes Left

There is no place to hide. Soon, molten lava will cover Earth's surface. I can't help but think that we are all going to die. I don't want to die; I have things I want to do in life!

Another three whole minutes until we are going to be covered in lava... All of the lights shut off. It's just a matter of time before I get hit by lava... but I don't. I watch the lava burn through the roof. I'm the only person to live on the Earth. Everything is covered in smoky, grey ash.

Lexi Reid (11)

Winterton Community Academy, Winterton

Eruption

In 1997, a little goat lived on the side of a volcano in the Philippines. One day, the volcano erupted and molten hot lava started to track its way down the side of the volcano. The little goat started to charge up closer to the active volcano. He made a huge mistake! Scorching boulders flew like birds through the sky and landed with a sizzling, piercing sound. As the goat got more scared, he ran closer to the scorching lava. A rock flew closer to the little goat until one was heading its way...

Sophie Jo Wright (12)

Winterton Community Academy, Winterton

Tainted Frost

I curled up in a tight ball, my deep blue skin becoming a frozen purple. The snow was still crashing down outside of my safe space, a shallow cave I had found. In my temporary state of calm, a clump of snow fell in the entrance. Moving to avoid the snow, I hit the wall of the cave with a loud thud. I wished I had taken up magic studies, then I could summon a small fire. Ignoring my instincts to just stay warm, I plunged my fist through the snow and a hand from the other side grabbed me...

Carys Scott (13)
Winterton Community Academy, Winterton

London's Crisis

I'm running. Beneath me, the ground is shaking and so am I. Looking around me, I feel a tear drop from my eye. What has happened to this place? My skin is pale and extremely cold. I'm on my own. London is in a state of horror. What was once a towering clock tower known as Big Ben, is now just a crumble of rocks on the floor. I get a notification telling people to evacuate but it is too late for me. Tears now stream down my face as my inevitable fate hits me. This could be the end.

Jack Lawrence (14)
Winterton Community Academy, Winterton

The Earthquake

Suddenly, I felt the ground was shaking. I was wondering what it was. I freaked out because it kept on shaking and my mum was at work and I asked her if she could feel the shaking. She said yes. I got my stool out to get into the loft but it was still shaking up there. I was so scared, so I rang my mum but she didn't answer. I was worried she wasn't there, so I ran to her work and the ground was crumbling behind me. I got really tired and I fell in...

Dylan Jones (11)
Winterton Community Academy, Winterton

YOUNG WRITERS INFORMATION

We hope you have enjoyed reading this book – and that you will continue to in the coming years.

If you're a young writer who enjoys reading and creative writing, or the parent of an enthusiastic poet or story writer, do visit our website **www.youngwriters.co.uk**. Here you will find free competitions, workshops and games, as well as recommended reads, a poetry glossary and our blog.

If you would like to order further copies of this book, or any of our other titles, then please give us a call or order via your online account.

Young Writers
Remus House
Coltsfoot Drive
Peterborough
PE2 9BF
(01733) 890066 / 898110
info@youngwriters.co.uk

Join in the conversation!

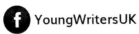 YoungWritersUK  @YoungWritersCW